tangled loyalties
The Protector Series
Book Three

viggo vaughn

Tangled Loyalties
The Protector Series - Book 3
Copyright © 2025 by Viggo Vaughn
All rights reserved.

Book Cover and formatting provided by Trisha Fuentes
https://bit.ly/m/trishafuentes

No part of this book may be reproduced in any form or by any electronic or mechanical means, including information storage and retrieval systems, without written permission from the author, except for the use of brief quotations in a book review.

ISBN: 979-8-3483-2629-6 (Paperback)

**Published by
Ardent Artist Books**
www.ardentartistbooks.com

about ardent artist books

➥ **ABOUT US**

Ardent Artist Books was established in 2008

We publish modern and historical romances once a month!

Get Your FREE List: Published & Upcoming Books
visit our website at:
https://bit.ly/3Wva4o0

* * *

➥ **WE HAVE BOOK TRAILERS**

Follow us on YouTube!
https://bit.ly/3W3xn7a

Like, Subscribe & Comment

* * *

➡ WE HAVE SERIALIZED FICTION!

Visit our website today to download one of our stories that unfold in bite-sized pieces!

Each installment is just 99¢!
Paperback $15.99

https://bit.ly/3LsDpJL

* * *

➡ LET'S CONNECT!

Fuel your love of fiction with exclusive content and captivating insights from Ardent Artist Books. Whether you crave the thrill of modern narratives or the timeless elegance of historical fiction, our newsletter delivers a curated selection straight to your inbox. Plus, as a welcome gift, receive a FREE downloadable eBook:

"The Family Fix"

https://bit.ly/49BR3UB

contents

Prologue	1
1. Elara Moretti, 18	11
2. Demand for Truth	19
3. The Safehouse	29
4. Defiance	39
5. The Moretti Threat	49
6. Metallic Taste of Blood	59
7. Wash Away the Grime	69
8. The Shower	77
9. Equal Upbringing	87
10. Walk of Shame	99
11. The Café	109
12. Escape the Warehouse	121
13. The Treaty	131
Epilogue	141

you might also like

The Dark Side of Him	151
Guarded by Shadows	153
The Bargain Bride	155
Second in Command	157
Evenly Matched	159
About Viggo Vaughn	161
Also by Viggo Vaughn	163

prologue
...

The bass from *Club Euphoria* still pulses through my veins as I step into the crisp night air. Amber - or was it Ashley? - slips her number into my pocket, her perfume lingering as she whispers promises of a wild night. Any other time, I'd be all over that invitation. But tonight isn't about pleasure.

I check my phone. Three clubs down, no sign of Elara Moretti. The photo I have of her doesn't do her justice according to my sources - they say she's a knockout with those signature Moretti blue eyes. My intel better be solid about her Friday night habits, or this whole operation goes sideways.

"You sure you don't want company?" Amber/Ashley calls from the club entrance, her voice carrying that perfect mix of suggestion and need that usually hits all my buttons.

I flash her my practiced smile, the one that makes women weak in the knees. "Rain check, beautiful. Business calls."

The disappointment on her face almost makes me reconsider.

Almost. But Enzo's life hangs in the balance, and Sofia Moretti needs to learn she can't fuck with our family.

My Audi purrs to life as I pull up the next location on my phone - *Club Venom*. The bouncer there owes me a favor, which might come in handy if Elara shows up. I navigate through downtown's maze of one-way streets, my mind racing through scenarios of how to approach her when I find her.

Too aggressive, she'll bolt. Too subtle, she might not take the bait. I need to play this perfectly - be the charming stranger who catches her eye but doesn't seem to know or care about her family connections. The kind of guy who makes her want to break her own rules.

The line outside *Venom* stretches around the block, but I park right up front. The privileged perks of being a Falchetti in this city. Women in the queue eye my car, then me as I step out. Their interest is obvious, but I barely notice. My focus narrows to the mission at hand.

Mike, the bouncer, gives me a slight nod as I approach. "Mr. Falchetti."

"Busy night?" I ask, slipping him an envelope thick with cash. "Need intel on someone who might show up."

His massive frame shifts closer, voice dropping. "Already here. VIP section, far corner. Wearing red."

My pulse quickens. Finally. I smooth down my jacket and head inside, the thrumming music washing over me. The crowd parts as I move through - there's something about the way I carry myself that makes people instinctively clear a path. Years of training, of knowing I'm untouchable in these spaces.

The VIP section rises above the main floor, offering a perfect view

Prologue

of the writhing masses below. I scan the elevated booths until I spot a flash of red. My breath catches.

The intelligence photos didn't do Elara justice at all. She's perched on the edge of her seat, laughing at something her friend is saying. That red bustier hugs every curve, her dark hair falling in waves past her shoulders. But it's her eyes that grab me - electric blue, just like they said, but with something soft and vulnerable in them that the photos couldn't capture.

For a moment, I forget why I'm here. Forget about Enzo, about Sofia, about the whole damn vendetta. I just want to know what makes this girl laugh, what thoughts swirl behind those striking eyes.

But then reality crashes back. She's a *Moretti*. A means to an end. Nothing more.

I make my way to the bar, positioning myself in her line of sight. Order a whiskey neat, though I won't drink it. Need my head clear tonight. I can feel her gaze land on me - women always look, and I've learned to sense it. But I don't acknowledge her yet. Let her wonder, let her interest build.

The bartender slides my drink over. I raise it slightly, taking in the amber liquid, aware of Elara's continued attention. Every move I make is calculated now, a careful dance of seduction and strategy. I've done this countless times before, but never with stakes this high.

The music shifts to something slower, more sensual. Perfect timing. I turn slightly, letting my eyes meet hers across the space between us. Hold the contact for three seconds - long enough to show interest, short enough to leave her wanting more. Then I look away, take a sip of my whiskey.

Elara moves through the crowd with an ethereal grace, her dark hair catching the strobe lights. But there's something else, something that makes my gut twist. She's clearly high, pupils dilated as she sways to the music.

I hang back in the shadows, watching her dance. She's uninhibited, sensual, moving between partners like she's searching for something she can't find. Male, female - it doesn't seem to matter. But beneath the drug-induced euphoria, I catch glimpses of desperation in her movements. The high is wearing off.

Mimo, my usual dealer contact, lurks near the bar. I make my way over, keeping Elara in my peripheral vision. "That's my sale tonight," I tell him, sliding several hundred across the counter. His eyes widen at the stack of bills, but he knows better than to argue with a Falchetti.

I position myself in a dimly lit corner, waiting. It doesn't take long. Elara approaches, her movements becoming more erratic as withdrawal sets in. Up close, she's even more striking - all delicate features and those striking blue eyes that pierce through me despite their drug-hazed state.

"Mimo said you could help me out," she says, her voice husky and uncertain.

My mouth goes dry. The physical pull between us is immediate and intense, catching me completely off guard. Heat floods my veins as she steps closer, her floral perfume mixing with the scent of sweat and vodka. This wasn't part of the plan. I'm supposed to be cold, calculating - not fighting the urge to run my fingers through her hair and taste those full lips.

"I've got what you need," I manage to say, but the words feel thick in my throat. Duty wars with desire as I watch her nibble

Prologue

her lower lip nervously. Christ, this job just got a lot more complicated.

I let my gaze drift over her, taking in every detail. The red bustier she wears accentuates her curves perfectly, and I have to force myself to stay focused. Her presence is magnetic, drawing me in despite my best efforts to maintain professional distance. My breath catches as she shifts closer, the strobe lights casting shadows across her delicate features.

"You're new," she says, tilting her head. Her voice carries a hint of suspicion beneath the need. "I haven't seen you here before."

I keep my expression neutral, though my pulse races. "I move around. Different clubs, different crowds." The lie falls easily from my lips, practiced and smooth. "But tonight, I'm right where I need to be."

She studies me with those striking blue eyes, and for a moment, I see a flash of clarity cutting through the drug-induced haze. There's intelligence there, sharp and assessing despite her current state. It catches me off guard - another complication I hadn't anticipated.

"I'm where I need to be, too," she says slurring her words and chuckling to herself. Her delicate fingers wrap around the glass in front of her, and I notice the slight tremor in her hand. The drugs are hitting her system hard - exactly what I need for this to work, even if something in my chest tightens at the sight of Elara Moretti so vulnerable.

I lean against the wall, letting the shadows play across my features. "First time I've seen you here," I say, keeping my voice low and inviting.

"I get around," Elara replies with a coy smile. She sways closer, and I catch another whiff of her expensive perfume beneath the club's heavy atmosphere. "Though I haven't seen you before either. I'd remember someone like you."

My heart hammers against my ribs. Even in her altered state, there's something magnetic about her - an innocent vulnerability that wars with a wild spark in those blue eyes. I force myself to remember why I'm here, what's at stake. Enzo's life depends on this working.

"Maybe we were meant to meet tonight," I say, letting my gaze drift over her face. Her pupils are wide, dark pools that can't quite focus. The responsible part of me wants to get her help, not exploit this situation. But I can't afford morals right now.

She leans in closer, her fingers brushing my arm. "Maybe we were." Her words slur slightly. "But unfortunately, I should probably go. I'm... out of funds for the evening."

This is my opening. I try to ignore how my stomach twists as I reach into my pocket, making sure she sees the small packet. "That doesn't have to be a problem. My car's right outside. We could continue this conversation somewhere more—private. Head for the coke?"

Elara's eyes lock onto the packet, and I see the internal struggle play across her features. Desire wars with hesitation. She bites her lower lip, and I find myself tracking the movement before I can stop myself.

"A blow job? I don't usually..." she starts, but her eyes never leave my hand.

"One second of bravery," I murmur, letting my free hand brush her waist. "That's all it takes. Let me take care of you tonight."

The rational part of my brain screams that this is wrong on so many levels. But when she looks up at me through those long

Prologue

lashes, I'm caught in a web of my own making. The mission blurs with genuine attraction, and I'm no longer sure where one ends and the other begins.

"Okay," she whispers, and steps closer. "Your car?"

I take her hand, ignoring how perfectly it fits in mine, how her touch sends electricity through my veins. As I lead her toward the exit, my mind races with the implications of what I'm about to do. The weight of the zip ties in my pocket feels heavier with each step.

Just before we reach the door, she squeezes my hand and pulls me to a stop. My heart freezes - has she sensed something's wrong? But when I turn, her eyes are soft with something that looks dangerously close to trust.

"I just wanted to say..." she starts, swaying slightly. "You seem different. Not like the others."

The words hit me like a physical blow. Because in this moment, as I lead her into a trap, I'm exactly like all the others who've taken advantage of her vulnerability. Maybe worse.

But I can't back out now. Enzo's life hangs in the balance. So I squeeze her hand back and give her my most reassuring smile, even as guilt churns in my gut.

"Let's go," I say softly, pushing open the club's door. The cool night air hits us like a wake-up call, and Elara shivers. Without thinking, I shrug off my jacket and drape it over her shoulders.

She looks up at me with those impossibly blue eyes, and for a moment, I forget to breathe. "Such a gentleman," she murmurs.

My car waits in the shadows of the parking lot, and with each step closer, my resolve weakens. The zip ties in my pocket feel like they're burning a hole through the fabric. Looking at her trusting face, I realize I've never hated myself more.

But before I can reconsider, she stumbles slightly on her heels. I catch her instinctively, and she falls against my chest with a soft laugh. Her warmth seeps through my shirt, and suddenly the night feels electric with possibility—and danger.

elara moretti, 18

...

The neon lights of *Club Venom* pulse through my veins, matching the frantic rhythm of my heart. I weave through the crowd, my designer heels clicking against the floor as bodies writhe and sway around me. The familiar itch crawls under my skin - I need another line.

The bass thumps through my bones as I scan the VIP section, searching for a familiar face who might have what I need. My sister Sofia would kill me if she knew I was here instead of attending another "family dinner." But that's the thing about being the black sheep - expectations are already so low, disappointing people becomes almost laughable.

"Hey sugar, looking for company?" Some sleazy guy in an expensive suit slides up next to me, reeking of cheap cologne and desperation.

I shoot him my deadliest glare. "Back off unless you want my sister's men to break both your kneecaps." The Moretti name still carries weight, even if I'm just the wayward little sister.

He pales and scrambles away. At least Sofia's iron-fisted leadership is good for something. Ever since Dad died last year, she's been running the family with ruthless precision, turning our already formidable operation into something truly terrifying. Meanwhile, I've been doing my best to stay out of it all, preferring the numbing embrace of cocaine and the pulsing rhythm of club music.

My hands shake slightly as I grab a champagne flute from a passing waitress. The high from my last line is wearing off. I down the bubbly in one gulp, remembering the first time I tried coke at sixteen. Some guard - Gio or Gerardo, I can't even remember now - offered it to me at a family party. The same guy I'd lost my virginity to the year before, thinking I was in love. God, I was such an idiot back then.

"Miss Moretti." Vincent, one of our regular dealers, materializes beside me. "The usual?"

I slip him some bills, and he passes me a small baggie. Simple, clean, professional - just like Sofia would want all our business dealings to be. The irony isn't lost on me that I'm supporting the family enterprise in my own fucked up way.

The bathroom is mercifully empty when I duck inside. I lean against the marble counter, studying my reflection in the gold-framed mirror. Same dark hair and blue eyes as Sofia, but where she radiates cold authority, I just look... lost. Whatever. I'm not here for self-reflection.

I cut a clean line on my phone screen with practiced ease. The powder disappears up my nose in one smooth motion, and I close my eyes as that familiar warmth spreads through my chest. This is what I'm good at - partying, rebelling, being everything a proper Moretti woman shouldn't be.

Elara Moretti, 18

My phone buzzes - another missed call from Sofia. She's probably sitting in her office right now, surrounded by our father's old ledgers and weapons, planning her next move against the Falchettis or some other rival family. She tries so hard to keep me in line, to mold me into someone worthy of the Moretti name. But I learned a long time ago that I'll never be that person.

The music calls to me as I exit the bathroom, my body already moving to the beat. Tonight isn't about family drama or criminal empires. Tonight is about losing myself in the chaos, about forgetting who I am and where I come from. Let Sofia have her throne of blood and bullets - I'll take the dance floor any day.

I spot a guy watching me from across the club, tall and dangerous-looking in a way that probably means he's connected. His eyes follow me as I start to dance, and I send him my most wicked smile. Maybe he's from a rival family. Maybe he works for Sofia. Maybe he's nobody at all. Right now, with cocaine singing in my veins and the music drowning out all thought, I couldn't care less.

Heat pools in my stomach as I move, remembering other nights like this one. That first time with the guard when I was fifteen, thinking I was so grown up, so in control. All the nameless faces since then, each one a middle finger to my family's expectations. Sofia probably has a file on every single one of them, cataloging my indiscretions like battle plans.

The guy is still watching me, and I let my movements become more provocative. This is what freedom feels like - or the closest thing to it I can find in this gilded cage of life. No responsibilities, no expectations, just the pure animal pleasure of being young and beautiful and completely out of control.

The lights blur and swim before my eyes as I scan the crowded club for Vincent. *Where the fuck did he disappear to?* My fingers drum against my thigh, that familiar itch crawling under my skin. The high is fading fast, leaving me hollow and desperate.

I shove my way through the mass of writhing bodies, ignoring the angry protests and wandering hands. The VIP section yields nothing but drunk businessmen and wannabe gangsters. No Vincent.

"Shit," I mutter, running a hand through my tangled hair. The music pounds against my skull, no longer euphoric but grating. I need another hit.

Movement near the bar catches my eye - someone passing small baggies to eager customers. Not Vincent, but at this point I don't care. I weave through the crowd, zeroing in on the dealer like a shark smelling blood.

He's younger than Vincent, with tattoos crawling up his neck and a dangerous glint in his dark eyes. "Looking for something, princess?" His accent is thick, Eastern European maybe.

"You know what I want." I pull out a wad of cash, not bothering to count it. "Make it quick."

"I'm Mimo." He grins, revealing a gold tooth. "New supplier for the area."

New supplier? Sofia would want to know about that. But the thought dissolves as he slips the baggie into my palm. *Who gives a fuck where he came from?* All that matters is the powder burning a hole in my hand.

I duck behind a column, away from prying eyes. My hands shake as I tap out a line on the back of my hand. The powder disappears up my nose in one practiced motion. The effect is instant - warmth spreading through my chest, my nerves settling like a cat curling up in the sun.

Elara Moretti, 18

The beat drops and I let it carry me back to the dance floor. My body moves on its own, liquid and free. *This is better. This is what I needed.* The lights paint patterns across my skin as I lose myself in the music, in the high, in the beautiful chaos of it all.

Every cell in my body vibrates with electric energy. I throw my head back, arms raised to the pulsing lights above. Let Sofia have her empire of blood and bullets. This is my kingdom - this perfect moment where nothing exists but the beat and the rush.

The guy from earlier is still watching me. His gaze burns against my skin, but I just close my eyes and keep dancing. Maybe he'll be tonight's mistake. Maybe he'll be the one that finally pushes Sofia over the edge. Maybe he'll be the death of me.

Right now, with cocaine singing through my veins and the bass drowning out all thought, I couldn't care less.

The euphoria starts slipping away like water through my fingers. My movements become jerky, desperate, as I try to hold onto that perfect high. But it's no use - reality comes crashing back in waves, each one hitting harder than the last.

"You okay, beautiful?" Some guy's hands settle on my hips, his breath hot against my neck. An hour ago, his touch might have sent pleasurable shivers down my spine. Now it just makes my skin crawl.

I shove him away without a word. The dance floor feels too crowded, too hot. Sweat trickles down my back, and my designer dress clings uncomfortably to my body. The lights that were so mesmerizing before now stab at my eyes like needles.

"Fuck," I mutter, scanning the club for Mimo. He was just here. Where the hell did he go? My fingers drum against my thigh as anxiety starts to claw at my chest. I need another hit. Now.

A couple grinding nearby bumps into me, spilling their drinks down my arm. "Watch it!" I snap, but my voice gets swallowed by the music. The sticky alcohol runs down my skin, and I swear I can feel every single drop. Everything's too much - too loud, too bright, too close.

I push through the crowd toward the bar, my movements growing more frantic. The bass that had me floating now pounds against my skull like a hammer. My heart races, but not in the good way anymore. This is the crash coming, and it's coming hard.

"Another champagne," I tell the bartender, trying to keep my voice steady. He slides the glass over, and I down it in one gulp. It doesn't help. Nothing helps except what I actually need.

I spot a flash of tattoos near the VIP section - Mimo? But when I get closer, it's just some random guy with similar ink. Disappointment hits me like a physical blow. Where's Vincent when you need him? He never disappears like this.

My phone buzzes again. Sofia's name flashes on the screen, along with six missed calls. *God, she's probably losing her mind right now!* I should answer, should at least let her know I'm alive. But the thought of hearing her voice, that mix of disappointment and barely controlled anger, makes me want to crawl out of my skin.

The lights keep flickering, faster and faster, matching the erratic beating of my heart. The music warps and distorts, transforming from rhythm to noise. I need to get out of here. I need another line. I need...

I stumble toward the bathroom, shoving past anyone in my way. My hands shake as I pull out my phone, checking the empty baggie one more time. There has to be something left. Even just a little bit. Just enough to take the edge off.

Elara Moretti, 18

But there's nothing. Just traces of powder that mock me with their inadequacy. I drop the baggie and grip the sink, staring at my reflection in the mirror. My pupils are blown wide, mascara smudged beneath my eyes. I look exactly like what I am - a mess. A disappointment. The wayward Moretti daughter who can't get her shit together.

The bathroom door opens, and two girls in tiny dresses stumble in, giggling and pulling out their own little baggies. My mouth goes dry at the sight. Maybe if I ask nicely... But no. I still have some pride left. Not much, but enough to stop me from begging strangers for drugs.

I splash some water on my face, trying to pull myself together. The cold helps, but only barely. Everything feels wrong - my skin too tight, my thoughts too loud, the world spinning just slightly off its axis.

I'm back in the thick of the crowd. My gaze darts between faces, searching for Mimo, *whatever the fuck his name was*. The bass thrums through my chest, and sweat beads on my neck despite the chill of my bare shoulders in my red cocktail dress.

No sign of Mimo. *Fuck.*

I press through to the VIP section, flashing a smile at the bouncer who knows my face, knows my family name. The velvet rope parts. Up here, the music softens enough for actual conversation, and the leather booths cradle the city's elite in shadowy privacy.

That's when I see him. Dark hair, sharp jawline, wearing a perfectly tailored suit that screams money. His hazel eyes catch mine from across the room, and my breath hitches. He's gorgeous in that dangerous way that my sister Sofia always warns me about.

I should look away. I don't...

demand for truth

...

elara moretti

The black cloth suffocates me, pressing against my mouth and nose with each panicked breath. My wrists burn from the plastic zip ties digging into my skin. The bastard caught me completely off guard—one minute I'm flying high, ready to blow this guy's knob in the car, the next I've got zip ties around my hands and in darkness. My heart races as I struggle against the restraints, my mind racing with questions. *What the hell is going on? Who is this guy? And why did he set me up like this?*

I can't believe my luck. Here I am, Elara Moretti, daughter of one of the most powerful crime families in the city, and I've fallen for some lowlife trick. But there's something about him that makes me think he's not just some random creep. He seems... professional. Like he knows what he's doing.

I try to focus on my surroundings, hoping to pick up any clues that might help me figure out where I am and what his plan is. The car is quiet except for the sound of my ragged breathing and the occasional rustle of fabric as I squirm against the zip ties. There's a faint smell of leather and cigarette smoke in the air, and I can hear the hum of the engine beneath us.

I can't see a damn thing with this blindfold on, but I can feel his presence nearby. His breath brushes against my ear as he speaks softly, his voice a mix of amusement and menace. "You really thought you could get away with that?"

My heart skips a beat at his proximity, and I swallow hard as fear grips me tightly. "Who are you?" I demand, trying to keep my voice steady despite my trembling body. "What do you want from me?"

He chuckles softly, his breath warm against my skin as he leans closer. "You don't need to know who I am," he says cryptically. "Just know that you're in deep trouble now."

I can't see him—but I can smell him—and he smells *good*. The rich scent of leather and something spicy, maybe sandalwood, wraps around me like an invisible embrace. It's intoxicating, dangerous, and against my better judgment, I find myself wanting to breathe deeper, to memorize this scent that screams power and masculinity.

My mind races as I try to come up with a plan to escape from this situation. But every idea that comes to mind seems impossible given my current predicament - bound and blindfolded in a moving car with an unknown assailant lurking nearby. Panic starts to set in as reality sinks in - I might not make it out of this alive.

But then something inside me snaps - a primal instinct for survival kicking into high gear. If there's one thing they didn't teach me growing up in the Moretti family, it was how to be helpless or give up easily. So instead of succumbing to fear or despair, I decide to fight back - both physically and mentally - no matter what it takes.

I start by wiggling my fingers against the zip ties binding my hands together, trying desperately to loosen them enough so that I can break free completely. It hurts like hell - those things are tight - but I refuse to give up or let him see how much pain I'm in. Instead, I grit my teeth and keep struggling until finally... there's a click! One of the zip ties has come undone!

With newfound hope coursing through my veins, I focus all my energy on freeing myself completely from these restraints before he realizes what happened and comes back for me again. My heart pounds loudly in my chest as sweat drips down my face from exertion - but finally... both zip ties have been removed!

Now all that remains is getting rid of this damn blindfold so that I can see where we are and figure out how to escape safely without alerting him or putting myself at further risk...

The car screeches to a halt, jolting me forward. I throw my hands out instinctively, bracing myself against the dashboard. My heart races as I fumble for the door handle, still blindfolded and disoriented. I can feel his eyes on me, watching my every move with amusement.

As I finally manage to pull the door open, a wave of cool air rushes in, sending a shiver down my spine. I try to stand up, but before I can even get my bearings, he's there, yanking me out of the car with a force that takes my breath away.

I stumble, my legs unsteady beneath me, but he doesn't let go. Instead, he pulls me closer, his grip tightening around my arm. I can hear him laughing softly, the sound sending a chill down my spine.

"You think you're so clever, don't you?" he says, his voice low and mocking. "You think you can just escape like that?"

I try to pull away, but he's too strong. I can feel the anger building inside me, burning like a wildfire. "Who the fuck are you?" I spit out, my voice raw and angry. "You think you can just grab me like this? You have no idea who you're dealing with!"

He chuckles again, the sound sending a shiver down my spine. "Oh, I know exactly who I'm dealing with," he says, his voice dripping with sarcasm. "Elara Moretti, the rebellious daughter of the great Salvatore Moretti. The girl who thinks she can do whatever she wants without consequences."

I feel a surge of panic at the mention of my father's name. *How does he know who I am? What does he want from me?*

Before I can even process these thoughts, I feel something sharp and cold against my wrists. He's zip-tying my hands behind my back again, the plastic biting into my skin. I try to struggle, but it's no use. He's too strong, and I'm too disoriented.

"Let me go!" I scream, my voice echoing in the darkness. "I swear to God, if you don't let me go right now, you'll regret it!"

He laughs again, the sound sending a chill down my spine. "Oh, I don't think so," he says, his voice low and menacing. "You see, I have plans for you, Elara. Big plans."

I feel a wave of fear wash over me, but I refuse to let him see it. Instead, I straighten up, trying to project an air of confidence that I don't feel. "What do you want from me?" I demand, my voice steady despite the trembling in my legs.

He doesn't answer right away. Instead, he leans in close, his breath hot against my ear. "You'll find out soon enough," he whispers, his voice sending a shiver down my spine. "But for now, let's just say that you're going to be very useful to me."

I try to pull away, but he's holding me too tightly. I can feel the anger building inside me, burning like a wildfire. I won't let him do this to me. I won't let him use me like this.

"Fuck you," I spit out, my voice filled with venom. "You can't do this to me. I won't let you."

He chuckles again, the sound sending a chill down my spine. "We'll see about that," he says, his voice low and menacing. "But for now, let's get going. We have a long night ahead of us."

With that, he starts to drag me towards something - I can't see what it is, but I can hear the sound of footsteps echoing in the darkness. I try to resist, but it's no use. He's too strong, and I'm too disoriented.

As we walk, I try to take in my surroundings, trying to figure out where we are and what's happening. But it's no use. The blindfold is too tight, and the darkness is too complete. All I can do is stumble along, trying to keep up with him as he drags me deeper into the unknown.

I don't know what's going to happen to me, but I know one thing for sure: I won't go down without a fight. I'll do whatever it takes to escape, to get back to my family and my life. I won't let him win.

But as we walk further and further into the darkness, I can't help but feel a growing sense of dread. *Who is this man? What does he want from me? And how am I going to get out of this alive?*

My heart pounds in my chest as I stumble along, trying to keep up with his brisk pace. The blindfold is still tight around my eyes, and the zip ties dig into my wrists, making it difficult to move. I can feel the cold air on my face, and I shiver involuntarily.

Deeper dread enters my stomach when I realize just how vulnerable I am now, alone with this stranger. What would he do with me? All sorts of bad thoughts enter my head: rape, drug overdose, death. I try to push them away, but they linger like a dark cloud over me.

I can hear the sound of his footsteps in front of me, and I try to match his pace. My legs feel like jelly, and I'm not sure how much longer I can keep going. I'm starting to feel lightheaded, and my breathing is becoming more labored.

Suddenly, he stops, and I almost run into him. I can feel his presence looming over me, and I shrink back, trying to put as much distance between us as possible.

"Where are you taking me?" I ask, my voice trembling.

He doesn't answer right away. Instead, I hear the sound of a door opening, and he pushes me forward. I stumble into the room, my heart racing. I can feel the cold concrete floor beneath my feet, and I shiver again.

"Sit down," he says, his voice cold and commanding.

I do as he says, my legs giving out beneath me. I can feel the rough surface of the floor against my skin, and I try to steady my breathing. I'm trying to stay calm, but it's getting harder and harder with each passing second.

I can hear him moving around the room, and I strain my ears, trying to make out what he's doing. I can hear the sound of metal clinking together, and I wonder if he's getting a weapon. My heart races even faster at the thought.

"What do you want from me?" I ask again, my voice barely above a whisper.

He doesn't answer right away. Instead, I hear the sound of a chair scraping against the floor, and then he's sitting down in front of me. I can feel his gaze on me, and it makes me feel even more vulnerable.

"I want you to listen to me very carefully," he says, his voice low and menacing. "You're in a lot of trouble, Elara. You've been playing a dangerous game, and now it's time to pay the price."

I swallow hard, trying to keep my voice steady. "What are you talking about?"

"You know exactly what I'm talking about," he says, his voice dripping with contempt. "You've been snooping around where you don't belong. You've been asking questions that you shouldn't be asking. And now, you've gotten yourself mixed up in something that you can't possibly understand."

I try to think back to what he could be talking about, but my mind is racing. *I've been careful, haven't I? I've been trying to stay out of trouble and keep a low profile. But maybe I've been too careless. Maybe I've let my guard down.*

"I don't know what you're talking about," I say, trying to sound convincing. "I don't know anything about any game."

He laughs, a cold, humorless sound. "You're a terrible liar, Elara. But that's okay. You don't have to tell me anything. I already know everything I need to know."

I feel a chill run down my spine at his words. *How could he know anything about me? I've been so careful.*

"What do you want from me?" I ask again, my voice trembling.

"I want you to be a good little girl and do exactly what I tell you," he says, his voice cold and commanding. "I want you to tell me everything you know about the Moretti family. I want you to tell me about their operations, their allies, their enemies. I want to know everything."

I feel a surge of anger at his words. *How dare he?* The Moretti family is my family. I would never betray them.

"I won't tell you anything," I say, my voice firm. "You can do whatever you want to me, but I won't betray my family."

He laughs again, a cold, cruel sound. "You think you have a choice? You think you have any power here? You're just a pawn, Elara. A pawn in a much larger game."

I feel a wave of fear wash over me at his words. *What does he mean? What game is he talking about?*

"I don't know anything about any game," I say, my voice trembling. "Please, just let me go. I won't tell anyone about this. I swear."

He doesn't answer right away. Instead, I hear the sound of him getting up from his chair. I can feel his presence moving closer to me, and I shrink back, trying to put as much distance between us as possible.

"You're right, Elara," he says, his voice low and menacing. "You don't know anything about the game. But you're about to find out."

I feel a hand on my shoulder, and I flinch involuntarily. He's standing right behind me now, his breath hot against my ear.

"You see, Elara, there are some things that are more important than power. More important than loyalty. More important than anything else in the world."

I feel a cold chill run down my spine at his words. *What could possibly be more important than family?*

"And what's that?" I ask, my voice barely above a whisper.

He leans in closer, his lips brushing against my ear. "Family," he whispers. "And I'll do whatever it takes to get my family back."

I feel a wave of fear wash over me at his words. *What does he mean? What is he planning to do?*

Before I can even process the thought, I feel a sharp pain in my arm. I cry out in surprise, trying to pull away, but it's too late. I can feel something cold and metallic being inserted into my vein, and then everything goes black.

the safehouse
. . .

elara moretti

When I come to, I'm lying on a cold, hard surface. My head is pounding, and my body feels heavy and sluggish. I try to sit up, but I can't seem to move. I can feel something holding me down, and I realize with a start that I'm strapped to a table. *Did they move me?*

Panic sets in as I struggle against the restraints, trying to break free. But it's no use. I'm completely immobilized.

I can hear the sound of footsteps approaching, and then he's standing over me. I can feel his gaze on me ... or are there more people in the room? The realization makes me feel even more vulnerable.

Just then, the blindfold falls away from one eye—and, I'm alone. All alone.

My vision swims as consciousness creeps back, bringing with it a barrage of sensations. The metal table beneath me bites into my skin, its surface unforgiving and clinical. My wrists and ankles burn where thick straps hold me down, and my muscles scream in protest as I test their strength.

"Fuck," I whisper, my throat raw. The word echoes in the stark room, bouncing off bare concrete walls. This isn't some random basement or warehouse – everything's too clean, too organized. The air carries the sharp bite of disinfectant mixed with cigarette smoke.

Voices filter through what must be a closed door, their words indistinct but their tone clear – male, authoritative, discussing something with practiced efficiency. My heart pounds faster as I count at least three different voices. Are they Falchetti soldiers? Or something worse?

A fluorescent light hums overhead, casting harsh shadows across my limited field of vision. To my right, metal shelving holds neat rows of supplies – gauze, tape, what looks like medical equipment. The sight makes my stomach turn. What the hell are they planning to do with that stuff?

My head throbs where they must have hit me. The last thing I remember is the drug dealer putting that bag over my head, his hands surprisingly gentle even as he zip-tied my wrists. The memory of his touch sends an unwanted shiver through me. *Stupid, stupid girl.* All that flirting, that chemistry – it was just part of his game.

I twist my wrists against the restraints again, feeling the padding beneath the straps. They know what they're doing. These people are professionals, not some amateur crew. That should terrify me more, but instead, a bitter laugh bubbles up in my throat. Of course, they're pros. They're the fucking Falchetti family.

The voices outside grow louder, footsteps approaching. I force my breathing to steady, though my pulse races wildly. Sofia would

The Safehouse

know what to do. My sister always knows what to do. But Sofia isn't here – I'm alone, strapped to a table in what feels like a military-grade medical facility.

"Keep it together, Elara," I mutter to myself, scanning the room again. Besides the shelving, there's a steel sink in one corner, its surface gleaming. A small window near the ceiling lets in a thin strip of natural light – basement level, then. The glass looks reinforced, too thick for escape even if I could reach it.

More footsteps in the hallway, different from before. These are measured, unhurried. Confident. The click of expensive shoes on concrete sends ice through my veins. This isn't some grunt coming to check on me – this is someone in charge.

I strain to hear the conversation outside the door:

"...condition stable..."

"...proceed as planned..."

"...father's orders..."

Father's orders? My mind races. Which father? Whose father? The Falchetti patriarch? The thought makes me want to vomit.

The antiseptic smell grows stronger, mixing with traces of coffee and cologne. This place feels lived-in, maintained. A safehouse, maybe, but a permanent one. The kind of place where people disappear.

I close my eyes, trying to focus. *Think, Elara. What would Sofia do?* My sister's voice echoes in my head: "Always work the angles. Find the weakness. Everyone has one."

But right now, strapped down and aching, my only angle is the harsh fluorescent light above me, and the only weakness I can find is my own stupid decision to trust a handsome stranger with dangerous eyes.

Metal scrapes against metal – a lock turning. I shake my head until the entire blindfold falls down and over my nose and mouth, forcing my face into what I hope is a mask of defiance. If they're going to break me, they'll have to work for it.

The door opens with a soft whoosh of hydraulics. More evidence of money, of permanence. This isn't some temporary holding cell – it's a facility built for purpose. The thought settles like lead in my stomach as fresh voices join the symphony of murmurs beyond the doorway.

Somewhere in the building, a phone rings. The sharp electronic tone cuts through the background noise, followed by quick footsteps and muffled conversation. This place is active, populated. *How many people are here? What kind of operation are they running?*

My fingers twitch against the restraints, seeking purchase, finding none. The padding might prevent marks, but it also makes it impossible to get any leverage. They've done this before. The thought circles in my mind like a vulture, picking at my remaining courage.

I hear a voice command in Italian – crisp, authoritative. The footsteps pause. My heart hammers against my ribs as I wait, every muscle tense. Someone important is about to walk through that door, and I have nowhere to run, nowhere to hide.

Two men walk in—and, what the fuck—they look like male models! The first thing I notice is *him*—the guy from the bar. The one who tricked me. His expression is unreadable now, a far cry from the seductive charm he wielded earlier.

But it's the other man who commands my attention. Tall, imposing, with features that could've been carved from marble - he radiates authority. The way he stands, the way the others defer to him... he's clearly in charge. Something about him sends chills down my spine.

"Miss Moretti." His voice is deep, controlled. "I trust you're comfortable?"

I want to spit in his face. Instead, I force a sardonic smile. "Oh yeah, being kidnapped is totally my idea of a good time."

He doesn't react to my sarcasm. "Tell me about your sister's operations."

"Fuck you." The words fly out before I can stop them.

His jaw tightens. "Let me be clear. Your situation here depends entirely on your cooperation."

"And let me be clear - I don't know shit about my sister's business, and even if I did, I wouldn't tell you." My voice shakes but I lift my chin, meeting his steely gaze.

The man from the bar - my betrayer - shifts uncomfortably beside his boss. I shoot him a venomous glare. "Nice act back there. Really had me fooled."

"Enough." The leader's voice cuts through the tension. "Your sister's recent movements. Her contacts. Start talking."

My heart pounds against my ribs. The Falchettis. These must be the fucking Falchettis. Sofia's warned me about them, though she never went into details. Now I understand why.

"I don't know anything," I say firmly. "Sofia doesn't share that stuff with me."

"You expect me to believe the head of the Moretti family keeps her own sister in the dark?" He leans closer, his presence overwhelming. "Try again."

"Believe whatever you want. I'm an artist, not a mobster. The only thing I know about Sofia's business is to stay the hell out of it."

His eyes narrow, searching my face for lies. I hold his gaze, even as fear courses through my veins. I'm not lying - Sofia's always kept that part of her life separate from mine. But would they believe that?

"Search her phone," he commands.

The guy from the bar pulls my phone from his pocket—when did he take it?—and starts scrolling through it.

"You won't find anything," I say. "But hey, enjoy my selfies and art references."

The leader's frustration is palpable now. He paces a few steps, then turns back to me. "Your sister is holding my brother hostage. I want him back."

"His brother?" The words tumble out before I can stop them. "What the actual fuck are you talking about?"

The leader's - Dante's - eyes narrow dangerously. "Don't play dumb. Your sister has my brother, Enzo. And now, we have you."

The reality hits me like a punch to the gut. This isn't about business or territory - it's about *family*. And I'm just a pawn in their twisted game. My stomach churns as pieces click into place. The secretive phone calls, Sofia's increased security, the tension in her shoulders whenever someone mentioned the Falchettis.

Fuck. My sister has his brother. Fuck me, why would she do that?

Movement catches my attention as the guy from the bar—the one who played me so perfectly—leans over. His fingers brush my neck as he removes the blindfold completely. That familiar scent washes over me—expensive cologne mixed with something darker, dangerous. My body betrays me, responding to his proximity despite everything. Heat floods my cheeks as I remember how easily I fell for his act at the bar, how willing I'd been to...

No. Focus, Elara.

I turn my head away from him, but not before catching the knowing glint in his eyes. Bastard.

"So what's your grand plan here?" I direct my question at Dante, keeping my voice steady despite the fear coursing through my veins. "Keep me tied up until Sofia trades your brother for me?"

"That depends entirely on your sister," Dante replies coldly. "And on how useful you make yourself in the meantime."

I bark out a laugh, harsh and bitter. "Useful? I already told you—I don't know anything about Sofia's business."

"Oh, but you do know some things," the guy from the bar interjects. His voice still holds that seductive edge that drew me in earlier. I hate how it affects me even now.

"Well, I don't," I snap. "Sofia made damn sure of that. She might be overprotective, but at least she never kidnapped anyone's sister."

Dante's expression darkens. "No, she just kidnapped my brother instead."

"And that's my fault how exactly?" I strain against the restraints, anger temporarily overriding fear. "I had no idea about any of this until two minutes ago!"

"Perhaps," Dante concedes. "But you're here now, and you're going to help us get him back."

"Or what?" The words come out challenging, even though my heart's threatening to burst from my chest.

"Mr. Falchetti." A new voice from the doorway. "The preparations are complete."

Falchetti. The name hits me like ice water. The man from the bar isn't just some soldier - he's a Falchetti too. The family that's been at war with mine for generations. The family Sofia warned me about in whispered conversations and stern lectures.

"What preparations?" My voice cracks slightly. "What are you planning to do?"

Dante's lips curve into something that might be a smile on anyone else. On him, it's pure menace. "That depends on you, Miss Moretti. Tell me—how far do you think your sister would go to keep you safe?"

The question hangs in the air like smoke, choking me with its implications. I think of Sofia—fierce, protective Sofia who once broke a guy's fingers for grabbing my ass at a club. Sofia, who apparently now has Dante's brother locked away somewhere.

"What are you going to do?" I ask again, unable to keep the tremor from my voice.

Dante steps closer, his presence overwhelming. "Simple. You're going to call your sister. You're going to tell her exactly what I say to tell her. And then..." He pauses, studying my face. "Well, that part's up to her."

defiance
...

sofia moretti

The weight of the gun feels familiar in my hand, its cold metal barrel an extension of my fury as I keep it trained on Mia's tear-streaked face. My finger rests against the trigger, each heartbeat pulsing through my body like electricity. The warehouse air hangs thick with the metallic scent of blood and gunpowder.

I've pictured this moment countless times - eliminating one of the pawns in my game against the Falchetti family. But now that it's here, something feels off. Wrong.

"The Falchetti have retreated! They took the girl!"

The shout from one of my men slices through my concentration. My grip on the gun tightens, knuckles whitening.

"What girl?" The words scrape past my lips.

"Your sister, Miss Moretti. They grabbed Elara at *Club Venom* last night."

The name hits me like a physical blow. Elara. My baby sister. The room spins for a moment as memories flash through my mind - Elara's defiant blue eyes, her artistic hands always stained with paint, her fierce independence that both infuriates and terrifies me.

My gaze darts to Enzo's unconscious form slumped against the wall, blood trickling from the gash on his forehead where I struck him with the pistol. The perfect hostage, rendered useless now that they have my sister. Bile rises in my throat as I realize how thoroughly I've been outplayed.

The gun suddenly feels heavier in my hands. I lower it slowly, my arm trembling with the effort of restraint. For a split second, my carefully constructed mask cracks. Fear seeps through—raw and consuming—as I imagine what they might do to Elara. *She's just a kid, for fuck's sake. She was never supposed to be part of this.*

But the vulnerability passes quickly, replaced by white-hot rage that burns away everything else. I whirl back to face Mia, who flinches at the hatred in my expression.

"This is all your fault," I spit the words at her. "You and your pathetic romance with that Falchetti bastard. Everything was under control until you came along." My voice rises with each accusation. "Now they have my sister because of you. Because of him. Because of this whole fucking family that's determined to destroy everything I care about!"

The last words echo off the warehouse walls, leaving behind a ringing silence broken only by Mia's quiet sobs and my own ragged breathing. My hands are shaking now, but not from fear. Pure, unadulterated fury courses through my veins like poison.

"First they take my father. Then my cousin Tony. And now my sister." I step closer to Mia, watching her shrink away. "The Falchettis are like a cancer, spreading their destruction through everything they touch. And you—" I jab a finger at her chest, "—you let them in. Welcomed them with open arms and spread your legs for one of their killers."

My emotions war inside me as memories of Dante flood back unbidden. That arrogant smirk, those dark eyes that used to look at me with such heat, the way his rough hands would trace my curves with surprising gentleness. *Damn him. Damn everything about him.*

"Get everyone in position!" I bark at my men, needing to focus on something besides the ache in my chest. "I want eyes on every Falchetti property within the hour."

Three years ago, things were different. I thought I had it all figured out - the perfect plan to unite our families through marriage. Dante and I were explosive together, passion and power intertwined. In those stolen moments between sheets in luxury hotel rooms, I'd whisper my dreams of joining our empires. He'd kiss me silent, but I felt his agreement in every touch.

What a fool I was.

I pace the warehouse floor, my heels clicking against concrete as I try to contain my rage. The gun feels heavier now as I slip it back into my thigh holster. My fingers brush against the small scar on my leg—a reminder of the night everything fell apart. The night Dante chose family loyalty over love.

"Sofia." One of my captains approaches cautiously. "What about the Ricci girl?"

Mia. I'd almost forgotten about her, huddled and trembling in the corner. My lip curls as I look at her tear-stained face. Just another pawn in this twisted game between families.

"Lock her up," I snap. "We might still need her."

The way Dante looks at me now—with cold hatred instead of burning desire—it tears at something deep inside me. Not that I'd ever let him see. I've perfected my mask of cruel indifference, learned to meet his glare with one of my own. But alone, in the dark of night, I remember how it felt to be loved by him.

"Miss Moretti." Another interruption. "We've got word on where they might be holding your sister."

My nails dig into my palms. "Tell me."

The old waterfront warehouse. Of course. Where else would that bastard take her? It's where Dante first kissed me, pushed me up against the rusty metal walls, and claimed my mouth like he owned me. Now he's holding my sister there, turning our memories into weapons.

"Get the cars ready," I order, straightening my jacket. "And someone clean up this mess."

I glance at Enzo's unconscious form. Such a pretty boy, so different from his brother. Dante was all sharp edges and barely contained violence. Enzo has a softness to him - one I plan to eliminate completely before this is over.

More memories surface as I watch my men drag him away. Dante's hands in my hair, his voice rough with need as he whispered Italian endearments against my skin. The way he'd look at me afterward, like I was something precious and dangerous all at once. The plans we made, the empire we dreamed of building together.

Then came that night. The night my cousin Tony died by Dante's hand, shattering any chance of peace between our families. I still remember the cold look in Dante's eyes as he told me it was over, that family came first. Always had, always would.

"Everything's ready, Miss Moretti."

I nod sharply, pushing away the echoes of the past. "Good. Let's show these Falchetti bastards what happens when they cross me."

But even as I move toward the door, my heart betrays me with whispered what-ifs. *What if things had been different? What if Dante had chosen me over family loyalty? What if we'd managed to build that empire together instead of tearing each other apart?*

* * *

mia ricci

My heart pounds against my ribs as Sofia's stilettos click away, fading behind the heavy metal door. The sound echoes through the warehouse, each step a reminder of how close I came to death. Her perfume—something expensive and floral—still lingers in the air, mixing with the musty concrete smell of my prison.

I close my eyes, trying to steady my breathing. *I wasn't dying today.* The zip ties bite into my wrists, but the chair beneath me isn't secured. Sofia's final words replay in my mind: "Lock her up tight. I'll deal with her later." But in her rush to leave, her men followed her out without securing me.

A rookie mistake. One that could cost them everything.

Voices drift through the thin walls—angry shouts and rushed commands. The sharp slam of car doors makes me flinch. My muscles tense as I strain to listen, picking up fragments of conversation.

"...need to move now..."

"...the sister..."

"...Falchetti's closing in..."

The warehouse falls silent. Too silent. My chance is now—maybe my only chance.

I test the chair, shifting my weight. It scrapes against the concrete floor, the sound impossibly loud in the empty space. I freeze, counting heartbeats, waiting for footsteps to come running. Nothing.

Working my hands against the zip ties, I feel the plastic dig deeper into my skin. The pain shoots up my arms, but I keep going.

More shouting outside. A car engine roars to life. They're mobilizing, probably heading wherever Sofia rushed off to. My window is closing.

I push myself up from the chair on shaky legs. The room spins for a moment—how long was I tied there? Hours? The concrete floor is cold under my bare feet. They took my shoes, probably to make running harder. Smart, but not smart enough.

The door looms before me, heavy steel with a push bar. This is it. If they left someone behind, I'm dead. If they locked it from the outside, I'm trapped. But I have to try.

The screech of tires fades into silence, leaving me alone with my thundering heartbeat in this dim warehouse. The musty air clings to my skin, heavy with dust and fear. My eyes fix on Enzo's still form sprawled across the concrete floor, and my chest constricts with each second he doesn't move.

Defiance

"Enzo?" My whisper echoes off the metal walls, unanswered.

I twist my wrists against the zip ties, and to my surprise, they give slightly. Sofia's men did a sloppy job—probably thought a waitress wouldn't know how to escape restraints. If they only knew about the self-defense classes I took after my parents died.

The warehouse looms around me, a maze of shadows and rusted shelving units. My mind races between the urge to run and the knowledge that I can't leave Enzo here. Not like this. Not with Sofia still out there, her threats hanging in the air like poison.

A glint catches my eye—a broken shelf with jagged metal jutting out at an angle. Perfect. I shuffle over, positioning the zip ties against the sharp edge. The metal bites into my skin as I saw back and forth, each movement bringing fresh pain, but I grit my teeth and keep going.

The plastic finally snaps, and I yank my hands free. Blood rushes back into my fingers with pins and needles, but I don't waste time rubbing feeling back into them. I rush to Enzo's side, dropping to my knees beside him.

His skin is cool under my trembling fingers as I cradle his head in my lap. A bruise is forming along his temple where they struck him, and dried blood crusts at the corner of his mouth.

"Enzo, please." I run my hands over his face, his chest, checking for other injuries. "You have to wake up. I can't do this alone."

Tears splash onto his cheeks as I lean over him. All the feelings I've been fighting surge up, impossible to contain anymore. "I love you," I whisper, the words catching in my throat. "Do you hear me? I love you, you stubborn, infuriating man. So you need to fight. Fight for us."

I pull him closer, trying to share my body heat, my fingers

tangling in his dark hair. His breath comes in shallow puffs against my arm, but he remains still. Too still.

"Please," I beg, rocking slightly. "Please don't leave me here alone."

A slight movement under my hands makes me freeze. His eyelids flutter, fighting to open. When they finally do, his gaze is unfocused, confused.

"Mia?" His voice comes out rough, barely above a whisper, but it's the most beautiful sound I've ever heard.

Our eyes lock, and the world narrows to just this moment—just us. His hand weakly finds mine, and I see everything I feel reflected in his dark eyes. Pain, fear, determination... love.

He starts to shift, trying to push himself up, when the rumble of engines cuts through the silence. Multiple vehicles, getting closer. My heart leaps into my throat as Enzo's expression hardens, both of us knowing what those sounds mean.

We're not safe yet.

the moretti threat

...

luca falchetti

The shadows dance across the safehouse walls like restless spirits, matching my own unease. I lean against the cold concrete, arms crossed, trying to maintain a facade of composure while my mind races. The events of the past few hours replay in an endless loop - Elara's defiant eyes, the softness of her skin as I bound her wrists, the way my heart skipped when she leaned in close before I betrayed her trust.

I watch Elara from across the room, studying her profile in the dim light. Even bound and angry, she carries herself with a grace that draws my eye. Her jaw is set in stubborn defiance, but I catch the slight tremor in her hands that betrays her fear. *Fuck. This isn't how I wanted things to go.*

"You need to eat something," I say, pushing a plate of food toward her. She turns her head away, those full red lips pressed into a tight line. The same lips that were inches from mine earlier today, before everything went sideways.

My fists clench at my sides. I'm supposed to be focused on the mission - getting information about the Moretti family, using her as leverage. Instead, all I can think about is how young and vulnerable she looks, despite her tough exterior. She's barely nineteen. Just a kid really, trying to act harder than she is.

"I'm not going to hurt you," I tell her softly. The words slip out before I can stop them.

She lets out a harsh laugh. "Right. Because kidnapping me was totally harmless."

I deserve that. But there's something in her voice—a crack in the armor—that makes my chest tighten. Behind the street-smart attitude and crude language, I glimpse flashes of the sheltered girl she must have been before life hardened her.

Moving closer, I crouch down to her eye level. "Listen, this isn't personal. It's just business." Even as I say it, I know it's a lie. It became personal the moment I saw genuine fear flash in those blue eyes.

"Fuck your business," she spits, but I catch how she shrinks back slightly when I lean in.

The protective instinct hits me hard and fast. I want to tell her it'll be okay, that I'll make sure no harm comes to her. Instead, I force myself to remember my role. Remember that she's Sofia Moretti's sister. Remember that at twenty-nine, I'm way too old to be having these thoughts about a teenager, no matter how mature she acts.

"The sooner you cooperate, the sooner this ends," I say, keeping my voice neutral even as desire and duty wage war inside me.

She tilts her chin up, defiant. A strand of dark hair falls across her face and my fingers itch to brush it away. "I'm not telling you shit about my family."

The loyalty in her voice twists something in my gut. She's protecting people who've already failed to protect her. I've seen the track marks on her arms, heard the rumors about her wild behavior. The Morettis let their youngest daughter spiral while they were busy with their empire.

"Your sister know about the coke?" I ask quietly. It's a low blow, but I need to maintain control of this situation. Of myself.

Color floods her cheeks. "Fuck you."

"That's what I thought." I stand up, needing distance from the pull of her. From the urge to gather her close and shield her from all of this - including myself.

Walking to the window, I stare out at the city lights. Behind me, I hear her shift in her chair, the zip ties creaking. Every cell in my body is aware of her presence, like a magnetic force I can't resist.

"You don't have to do this," she says suddenly, her voice softer. "You seem... different from them."

The words hit too close to home. I am different—or at least I thought I was before today. Before I kidnapped an innocent girl because my family ordered it. Before I started feeling things I have no right to feel.

"You don't know anything about me," I reply roughly.

"I know you haven't hurt me. Yet." There's a challenge in her tone that makes me turn back to face her. She's watching me intently, those blue eyes seeing too much.

"Don't mistake business for kindness," I warn, but my voice lacks conviction. Because she's right—I can't bring myself to hurt her. The thought of anyone hurting her makes my blood boil.

She leans forward slightly, and even though she's bound, there's a power in her posture that commands attention. "Then what should I mistake it for?"

The question hangs in the air between us, loaded with implications I can't afford to consider. I'm her captor, she's my prisoner. Any other narrative is dangerous—for both of us.

Fuck. I can't afford these thoughts. Not now. Not about her.

The door swings open with a metallic groan, and Dante's broad frame fills the entrance. One look at his face tells me everything I need to know—the storm brewing in his eyes speaks volumes before he even opens his mouth. My stomach tightens as he steps inside, his usual iron control showing hairline cracks.

"Our men are back from the raid on the Moretti warehouse," he says, voice sharp enough to cut glass.

I straighten, pushing off the wall. "And?"

"We killed several of their men. None of ours were lost." The words should taste like victory, but they're ash in the air between us. The unspoken truth hangs heavy—Enzo wasn't there. Another dead end.

Dante's jaw clenches as he continues the report, each word measured and precise despite the tension rolling off him in waves. I watch his hands, the way his fingers flex and curl—a tell he's never managed to eliminate completely. Whatever's coming next, it's worse.

"Sofia knows we have Elara." His eyes flash dark with barely contained rage. "She's furious. This could mean war."

"Shit." The word escapes before I can stop it. My fists clench at my sides as I process the implications. I've seen Sofia Moretti's handiwork firsthand—the bodies she's left behind, the empires she's toppled through manipulation and cunning. She's a cobra waiting to strike, and we've just given her the perfect reason.

"We need to take Elara somewhere safe," Dante declares, his gaze hardening to steel. "The underground casino."

My heart stutters. The casino is our strongest holdfast, a labyrinth of secrets and security that's never been breached. But it's also a powder keg of volatile personalities and dangerous games. The thought of taking Elara there, of exposing her to that particular brand of darkness...

"But Dante—"

I clench my jaw as Dante waves off my concerns, his dismissal hitting me like a physical blow. The underground casino? It's a powder keg waiting to explode, and I'm about to throw Elara right into it.

"No buts, Luca. We're out of options." Dante's voice drops low, dangerous. "We need her close, but hidden. She'll be safer there."

My fingers curl into fists at my sides. The logical part of my brain knows he's right—the casino is a fortress, protected by layers of security and secrecy. But the thought of taking Elara there, surrounding her with the worst of our world... "Dante—"

"This isn't a debate." He cuts through my protest like a blade. "You're taking her there. It's an order."

The words land heavy between us. Family or not, when Dante gives an order, we follow. It's been that way since we were kids, since the day I gave up my law career to help him. But for the first time, that iron-clad loyalty feels like chains around my chest.

I glance at Elara, still trembling slightly from everything that's happened. Her chin is lifted defiantly despite her fear, dark hair falling in waves around her face. Something twists in my gut when our eyes meet. She's beautiful in her rebellion, a flame that refuses to be extinguished even in the darkest moments. The pull I feel toward her is dangerous - more dangerous than any threat from the Moretti family.

My heart pounds against my ribs as I gather her few belongings. Each beat feels like a warning, reminding me that this attraction could be my undoing. I've spent years building walls around myself, protecting the family's interests with cold precision. But one look from her threatens to burn it all down.

"We need to go, Elara." I keep my voice steady despite the storm raging inside me. "It's not safe here."

"I'm not going anywhere with you." Elara's words cut through the tension, sharp as a blade. She crosses her arms over her chest, the sequins of her dance club top catching the dim light. "If I have to leave, I want someone else to take me."

I bite back a smirk. She's trying to wound my pride, but she doesn't realize how much worse the alternatives could be. My cousin Dante might be family, but he lacks the patience to handle someone like her. And the other men? I wouldn't trust them within ten feet of her.

"That's not happening." I keep my voice level, measured. Years of negotiating deals have taught me the value of staying calm when others try to provoke you. "I don't trust anyone else with your safety."

She scoffs, tossing her dark hair over her shoulder. The movement sends another wave of her perfume my way—something sweet and intoxicating that makes my pulse quicken. "My safety? You're the one who kidnapped me."

"And yet here you are, unharmed." I step closer, close enough to see the slight tremor in her hands despite her brave front.

"Which is more than I can guarantee if someone else takes charge of you."

My eyes trail over her against my will. The club outfit leaves little to the imagination—a sparkly red bustier and high-waisted shorts that show off long legs. But beneath the glamour, I notice the goosebumps on her arms, the slight shiver she's trying to hide. She needs a shower, clean clothes, a chance to wash away the night's events.

The thought of her in the shower sends my mind places it shouldn't go. I clench my jaw, forcing those images away. This isn't about attraction. It can't be. She's a means to an end, leverage against the Moretti family. Nothing more.

"Look at me." I wait until her blue eyes meet mine. "You need to clean up, change clothes. The casino has private suites. You'll be comfortable there."

"Comfortable?" She laughs, but there's no humor in it. "In a den of criminals and killers?"

"In a secure location where no one will dare touch you." I step even closer, close enough that she has to tilt her head back to maintain eye contact. "Because they know you're under my protection."

The air between us crackles with tension. I see the moment her pupils dilate, hear the slight catch in her breath. She affects me just as much as I affect her, and we both know it. It's a dangerous game we're playing.

"Your protection?" She practically spits the words, but I catch the underlying tremor in her voice. "Like I'm supposed to believe you care what happens to me?"

I should step back. Should put distance between us before this tension ignites something we can't control. Instead, I find myself reaching out, brushing a strand of hair from her face. Her skin is soft under my fingertips, and she doesn't pull away.

"Believe what you want." My voice comes out rougher than intended. "But right now, I'm your best option for survival."

She swallows hard, and I watch the movement of her throat, fighting the urge to trace it with my fingers, my lips. The attraction burns through my veins like fire, threatening to consume my carefully maintained control.

"Fine." She finally breaks eye contact, wrapping her arms around herself. "But I want real clothes. And a phone call."

"Clothes, yes. Phone call, no." I force myself to step back, to remember why she's here. "The casino has shops. You can choose whatever you need."

"With what money?" Her chin lifts defiantly.

"My money." I pull out my wallet, removing a black credit card. "Consider it part of your protection package."

She eyes the card like it might bite her. "I don't want your blood money."

"Then freeze." I shrug, though the sight of her shivering sends an unwanted pang through my chest. "Your choice."

The air between us crackles with tension. I want to tell her it'll be okay, that I'll protect her no matter what comes. But the words stick in my throat. *How can I make promises when every instinct screams that I'm already in too deep?*

metallic taste of blood
...

dante falchetti

The world spins like a twisted carousel as my men race through the city streets. Every turn of the wheels sends lightning bolts of pain through my side. I press my hand against the wound, feeling the sticky warmth of blood seeping between my fingers. The leather seats squeak beneath me as Mario takes another sharp turn.

Stupid. So fucking stupid.

My shoulder throbs with each breath, a stark reminder of my arrogance. I've gotten too comfortable, too confident in my position. The mighty Dante Falchetti, brought down by a single bullet because I couldn't be bothered to check my corners.

"Boss, stay with me." Mario's voice cuts through the haze of pain. His knuckles are white on the steering wheel as he weaves through traffic.

The metallic taste of blood fills my mouth where I've been biting my cheek. Years of training, countless missions, and I let my guard down for one fucking second. That's all it took. One of Sofia's men, lurking in the shadows like the rats they are, waiting for the perfect moment.

I didn't even see the bastard. Just felt the impact, like being hit by a sledgehammer. The force knocked me back, and suddenly I was staring up at the night sky, wondering what the hell just happened.

"We need to get you to the doctor." Tommy, sitting next to me in the back, presses another cloth against my shoulder. I grunt at the pressure. "That's a lot of blood, boss."

My men. They moved like a well-oiled machine the moment I went down. The air exploded with gunfire as they formed a protective circle around me, their bodies becoming a human shield. I could hear their shouts, their coordinated movements as they returned fire, covering each other while dragging me to safety.

"I'm fine," I growl, even as another wave of dizziness washes over me. The car swerves again, and I bite back a groan. "Just get us somewhere safe."

Pride is a dangerous thing in our world. I've always known that, preached it even. Yet here I am, paying the price for my own hubris. The Falchetti name made me feel untouchable, invisible. What a wake-up call.

Through the tinted windows, I watch the city blur past. *My city*. The empire I've helped build and protect. And in one moment of carelessness, I nearly lost it all. If that bullet had been a few inches to the left…

"They knew we'd be there," Tommy says, his voice tight with anger. "Someone talked."

He's right. The ambush was too well-planned, too precise. The thought sends a fresh surge of rage through my system, momentarily drowning out the pain. We have a rat in our ranks, and when I find them...

The car jerks as Mario takes another corner at high speed. My vision swims, black spots dancing at the edges. I force myself to focus, to stay alert. I can't show weakness, not even now. Especially not now.

"Call ahead," I order through gritted teeth. "Make sure the doc is ready. And get the Capo on the phone. He needs to know."

My father. The thought of facing him like this, of admitting my mistake, burns worse than the bullet wound. He taught me better than this. Always be vigilant, always expect betrayal. Basic lessons I forgot in my complacency.

The cloth Tommy's holding is soaked through now, the dark red a stark contrast against his pale hands. My own fingers are sticky with blood where they're pressed against my side. Each breath sends fresh waves of pain radiating from the wound.

"Almost there, boss," Mario calls from the front seat. His eyes meet mine in the rearview mirror, filled with concern and barely contained fury. "Five minutes tops."

Five minutes. I lean my head back against the seat, trying to steady my breathing. The adrenaline is wearing off, making the pain sharper, more insistent. But my mind is clearer now, already planning our next moves.

Sofia Moretti thinks she's won something today. Thinks she's proved a point by catching me off guard. But she's just signed her own death warrant. When I recover—and I will recover—I'm going to show her exactly why the Falchetti name carries so much weight in this city.

"Tommy," I manage, my voice rougher than I'd like. "Get word to our people. I want eyes on every Moretti operation within the hour. Every safehouse, every business front. If they so much as sneeze, I want to know about it."

The familiar iron gates of the Falchetti mansion emerge through the tinted windows. Home. Sanctuary. Prison. It's all of these things and none of them. The tires screech against the pavement as we skid to a stop, and the sudden jolt sends fresh waves of agony through my body.

"Get him inside!" Mario's voice booms across the courtyard. "Now!"

Hands grab me, steady and strong, lifting me from the blood-stained leather. I try to stand, to show some semblance of the strength expected from a Falchetti, but my legs betray me. The world tilts dangerously.

"I can walk," I insist, even as my vision blurs. The words come out slurred, unconvincing even to my own ears.

The marble floors of the mansion pass beneath me in a dizzying blur. Family portraits watch from the walls—generations of Falchetti men who bore this burden before me. Did they ever feel this vulnerable? This human?

"Keep your eyes open, boss," Antonio commands, his voice tight with concern. "Stay with us."

I try to respond, to give orders, to maintain control, but the words stick in my throat. The ceiling above me seems to pulse and swim, the ornate chandelier multiplying before my eyes. My father's voice echoes in my head: "A Falchetti never shows weakness." But right now, the darkness is winning.

Then I hear her voice, cutting through the chaos like a blade.

"What happened?"

Lila. Her footsteps race across the marble floor, and even through my fading vision, I catch the flash of concern in her eyes. She shouldn't be here, shouldn't see me like this. Yet something in my chest loosens at her presence.

"Dante?" Her hand finds mine, warm and steady. "Oh God, there's so much blood."

I want to tell her I'm fine, that this is nothing, that a Falchetti doesn't fall so easily. But the words won't come. Her fingers tighten around mine, and for a moment, that touch is the only thing anchoring me to consciousness.

"Get the doctor," she orders, her voice carrying a strength I didn't expect. "Now!"

Even as the darkness creeps in at the edges of my vision, I feel a surge of pride. This woman, who once seemed so out of place in our world, now commands my men with the authority of a born leader. The irony would make me laugh if it didn't hurt so damn much.

* * *

lila rossi

My heart pounds against my ribs as I watch Dante's men carry him through the mansion's grand entrance. Blood stains his expensive suit, and his usual commanding presence has been replaced by an unsettling vulnerability that makes my stomach twist.

"What happened?" The words tumble from my lips before I can stop them. No one answers, their faces grim as they lay him on the marble floor. I drop to my knees beside him, not caring about the blood seeping into my dress.

"Dante, stay with me." My voice cracks as I lean over him, searching his face for signs of consciousness. His skin is pale, too pale, and his breathing comes in shallow gasps.

His eyes flutter open, and a faint smile tugs at his lips. "I'm not going anywhere." The words come out rough, strained, but they send relief flooding through me.

I examine the makeshift bandage wrapped around his torso, now soaked through with crimson. "Once the doctor checks you out, I'll take care of you." My fingers brush against his arm, wanting to offer comfort but afraid of causing more pain.

Something shifts in his expression - a softening I rarely see. Despite his obvious agony, he seems to relax slightly at my words, as if my promise alone can shield him from the darkness threatening to pull him under.

But even now, even bleeding on his own floor, his mind turns to business. "Make sure the package is secure," he orders, his voice barely above a whisper but carrying that unmistakable authority that makes his men snap to attention.

They exchange knowing looks, nodding their understanding. I've been around long enough to know they're talking about Elara, though the specifics of her situation remain a mystery to me.

"Luca is handling it," one of them reports, and I feel some of the tension leave Dante's body. His trust in his cousin runs deep, and knowing Luca has things under control seems to give him permission to finally let go.

The doctor bursts through the door, medical bag in hand, and immediately starts barking orders. I begin to move away, giving him space to work, but Dante's hand catches my wrist with surprising strength.

"Stay by my side, please," he murmurs, his eyes growing unfocused. "Stay with me always—be my wife."

My breath catches in my throat as his grip loosens and his eyes close. The proposal hangs in the air between us, unexpected and overwhelming, as he slips into unconsciousness. I remain frozen beside him, my mind spinning with the weight of his words and the fear of losing him before I can give my answer.

My hands tremble as I watch the doctor work on Dante, his skilled fingers moving with practiced efficiency. The words echo in my mind: "Be my wife." *How many times has he asked me now? Three? Four?* Each time before, the question sent ice through my veins, made me want to run far from this dangerous world of his.

But this time feels different. The sight of him lying here, vulnerable yet still commanding, makes everything crystallize with startling clarity. I think of all the moments that led us here - the way he protected me from the beginning, how he showed me the beauty in his family's traditions, the fierce loyalty that binds them all together.

I squeeze his limp hand, careful to avoid the IV line. "You can't just propose and pass out, you know." My whisper carries a hint of the laugh I'm holding back, masking the fear still gripping my heart.

The doctor mutters in Italian as he works, words I've started to understand after months in this household. The bullet missed major organs. Dante will recover. My relief comes out in a shaky breath, and I sink deeper into the chair beside his bed.

I think about the first time I saw the Falchetti family together - how intimidating they seemed, all sharp edges and dangerous grace. Now I see the love beneath their harsh exterior. The way Giovanni's eyes soften when he speaks of his sons. How Enzo and Dante bicker but would die for each other without hesitation. Even Luca, with his calculated distance, shows his devotion through unwavering protection of those he considers family.

And somehow, without meaning to, I've become part of this intricate web. I belong here, among these people who understand that love and loyalty are worth killing for. Worth dying for.

The hours crawl by as I wait for Dante to wake. I practice the words in my head, turning them over like precious stones. *Yes. I'll marry you. I want to be your wife.* Each version feels simultaneously too simple and too profound for what I want to express.

A slight movement draws my attention. Dante's fingers twitch against mine, and his eyes flutter open. He blinks slowly, confusion giving way to recognition as his gaze finds mine.

"You're still here," he rasps, voice rough from the anesthesia.

"Always." I lean closer, brushing my thumb across his knuckles. "And speaking of always..." My heart pounds so hard I wonder if he can hear it. "You asked me something earlier. Before you passed out."

His brow furrows slightly, trying to remember through the haze of pain and medication. "Did I?"

"You did." I take a deep breath, steadying myself. "And this time, I have an answer for you." I meet his dark eyes, seeing the moment understanding dawns in them. "Yes, Dante. I'll marry you. I want to be Mrs. Falchetti - your wife, part of this family. All of it."

His grip on my hand tightens, and something fierce and possessive flashes across his face. "Say it again."

"Yes." I lean down, pressing my forehead to his. "Yes, I'll marry you."

wash away the grime
...

elara moretti

The one-way mirrors stretch before me like a funhouse maze, each pane reflecting my disheveled appearance back at me while letting the Falchetti men spy on their wealthy patrons. My captor's hand rests firm on my lower back, guiding me through the hidden corridor. His touch burns through my thin shirt, a constant reminder that I'm at his mercy.

"Move," he commands, his voice low and dangerous. The same voice that charmed me earlier now sends ice through my veins.

I catch glimpses of myself in the mirrors—dark hair wild from struggling, blue eyes wide with a mix of fear and defiance. Beyond the glass, I see the real show: men and women dressed in their finest, throwing away fortunes at the poker tables and roulette wheels. Their laughter and excited shouts filter through, mocking my situation.

A woman in a white sequined dress throws her head back, squealing as she wins another hand. I press my palm against the glass, wondering if anyone would notice if I screamed. But I know better. These people are here for the thrill of gambling with the mob. They wouldn't lift a finger to help me, even if they could hear me through the soundproof barrier.

"Don't even think about it," he warns, reading my thoughts. His fingers dig deeper into my back, steering me toward a concealed staircase.

The deeper we descend, the louder the bass becomes. The familiar thump of club music pulls at something primal inside me. It's *my* music, my escape. The beat matches my racing pulse, and suddenly my body aches for more than just freedom. I need that familiar rush, that powder-white embrace that makes everything float away.

I glance at my captor from the corner of my eye. His jaw is set, but there's a glint in his expression that tells me he's no stranger to the party scene. "Got any blow?" The words slip out before I can stop them.

He raises an eyebrow, his step faltering for just a moment. "Didn't expect that from you, princess."

"Don't call me princess." I curl my lip. "And don't act surprised. I've been clean for what, twelve hours now? Thanks to you and your zip ties."

The music grows louder as we reach the bottom of the stairs. The vibrations rattle through my bones, awakening that desperate need. My fingers twitch, remembering the familiar motion of cutting lines on glass tables in VIP rooms not so different from this one.

"You know I'm right," I press on, emboldened by desperation. "I can tell you're holding. Probably right pocket, little baggie with enough to keep you sharp but not sloppy."

His grip tightens, and he spins me to face him. His hazel eyes bore into mine, searching. "You're more observant than you let on."

"I'm more everything than I let on." I meet his gaze, refusing to back down. The need crawls under my skin like fire ants. "Come on, what's the harm? You've already kidnapped me. Might as well make it a party."

His free hand slides into his pocket, and I catch the flash of white powder in a small plastic bag. My heart races faster, pupils dilating at just the sight of it. He holds it up between us, just out of reach.

"This what you want?" His voice drops lower, dangerous and tempting all at once.

"You know it is." I lick my lips, eyes locked on the bag. The music pulses around us, and I can almost taste the bitter drip at the back of my throat.

"And what would your sister say?" He steps closer, his breath hot against my ear. "Sofia Moretti's baby sister, begging for coke from her kidnapper?"

The mention of Sofia snaps something inside me. "Fuck Sofia," I spit the words. "She doesn't own me. And neither do you."

The bag disappears back into his pocket as quickly as it appeared. "No," he agrees, "but I do control whether you get what you want. And right now, I need you clear-headed."

"You suck, you twisted bastard," I say, yanking my arm away from his grip.

"This way," my captor says, his hand firm on my lower back as he guides me into a private elevator. The doors slide shut with a soft ding, and my stomach drops as we descend. I study his reflection in the polished metal walls—jaw clenched, eyes forward, completely unreadable. *How can someone so dangerous make me feel so...safe?*

The suite takes my breath away when we enter. It's nothing like the cold cell I expected. Warm lighting bathes cream-colored walls, and plush carpeting cushions my feet. A king-sized bed dominates one room, draped in rich fabrics that probably cost more than my car.

"This is where you'll stay," he says, his voice oddly gentle. "There's everything you need—clean clothes, toiletries, food will be brought regularly."

I wrap my arms around myself, suddenly very aware of how disheveled I must look. "A gilded cage is still a cage."

"You need to shower." His nose wrinkles slightly. "You smell like that warehouse."

"I'm fine," I snap, though I know he's right. I probably reek of fear and concrete dust.

"This isn't a request." The suit steps closer, and my breath catches as his hands move to the buttons of my blouse. "You're filthy, and I won't have you ruining the furniture."

"What are you doing?" I try to step back, but his presence fills the room, overwhelming my senses. His fingers work quickly, professionally, but each brush against my skin sends electricity coursing through me.

"Taking care of a stubborn prisoner who doesn't know what's good for her." There's a hint of amusement in his voice as he unclips my red bustier from the back.

My heart hammers against my ribs. I should fight this, should be outraged, but something in his touch breaks through my defenses. The gentleness behind his efficient movements makes my knees weak. His hands are warm against my skin, and I find myself leaning into his touch despite every rational thought screaming at me to pull away.

"I can undress myself," I whisper, but there's no conviction in my voice. My body betrays me, responding to his proximity with a shiver that has nothing to do with the cool air on my skin.

His eyes meet mine, dark with an intensity that steals my breath. "Can you? Because so far you've fought me on everything else."

I open my mouth to argue, but no words come. He's right—I've been difficult, defiant, trying to maintain some control in a situation where I have none. But now, with his hands on me, that defiance melts away like snow in summer.

I catch myself staring at his hands as they work the buttons of my corset. Strong hands, capable of both violence and surprising gentleness. My breath hitches as his knuckles brush against my collarbone, and I find myself wondering what those hands would feel like tangled in my hair.

"You're very good at this," I murmur, letting my voice drop to a sultry whisper. "Undress many prisoners?"

He doesn't respond, but I notice the slight tightening of his jaw. Good. He's not as immune as he pretends to be.

"You know," I continue, swaying closer, "if you wanted to get me naked, you could have just asked."

His hands pause for a fraction of a second before resuming their task. "This isn't a game, Miss Moretti."

"Everything's a game." I reach up, wrapping my arms around his neck. The muscle there is solid, warm. "And I'm very good at playing."

His breath catches—I feel it against my cheek. For one electric moment, I think I've won. Then his hands grip my wrists, firmly peeling my arms away from his neck. "No."

The rejection stings, but I refuse to let it show. Instead, I step back, maintaining eye contact as I slowly peel off my blouse. "Your loss." The fabric whispers as it falls to the floor. My skirt follows, pooling at my feet like spilled ink.

I arch an eyebrow at him, daring him to look away. He doesn't. His gaze remains steady, professional, but I catch the slight flare of his nostrils, the way his fingers curl into fists at his sides.

"Still nothing?" I taunt, reaching for the clasp of my bra. "Not even a little tempted?"

Instead of answering, he moves past me in two quick strides. The shower springs to life with a hiss of water. Before I can react, his hands are on my shoulders, propelling me forward.

"Hey!" I yelp as he pushes me into the shower stall, clothes and all. The water hits me like a shock, instantly soaking through my remaining clothes.

"Shower," he commands, voice tight with something that might be frustration or amusement—I can't tell which. "You have fifteen minutes."

The door clicks shut behind him, leaving me alone with the steam and my wounded pride. I lean against the tile wall, letting the hot water run down my face. Despite everything, a smile tugs at my lips. He might have won this round, but I saw the desire in his eyes before he pushed me away.

Wash Away the Grime

The game isn't over. Not by a long shot.

I peel off my soaked clothes, tossing them over the shower door with a wet splat. "You're missing quite a show in here," I call out, loud enough to carry over the water.

"Fourteen minutes," comes his clipped response.

I laugh, tilting my face up into the spray. My captor might be playing hard to get, but I've never been one to give up easily. And judging by the way his hands lingered on my skin, by the darkness I saw flash in his eyes—he's not as immune to me as he pretends.

The water runs in rivulets down my body, washing away the grime of the warehouse but doing nothing to cool the fire burning under my skin. I close my eyes, remembering the strength in his hands, the heat of his body so close to mine.

"Thirteen minutes," his voice cuts through my thoughts, all business and control.

I smile to myself, reaching for the shampoo. Let him think he's won this round. We both know this is just the beginning. After all, I've always loved a challenge, and he might just be my most intriguing one yet.

The expensive shampoo smells like jasmine and something darker —sandalwood maybe. I work it through my hair, making sure to moan just loud enough for him to hear. "Mmm, this feels amazing."

His silence speaks volumes, and my smile widens. I might be his prisoner, but that doesn't mean I can't make him squirm a little. And judging by the tension radiating from the other side of that door, I'm definitely getting under his skin.

The game is on, and I plan to enjoy every minute of it.

the shower
. . .

elara moretti

Hot water cascades down my body, washing away the grime and tension of this hellish night. The shower's steady rhythm drowns out my racing thoughts, if only for a moment. Steam fills the luxurious bathroom, fogging up the glass walls. Even in captivity, the Falchettis spare no expense.

My mind drifts back to last night, replaying every moment that led me here. If only I'd listened to that nagging voice in my head telling me to stay home. But no—I had to prove I could have a life outside Sofia's suffocating protection.

> I'll be there at ten, E! We'll make it a night to remember!

Vanessa's text flashes through my memory, making my blood boil. Some friend she turned out to be. I waited at *Club Venom* for two hours like an idiot, checking my phone every five minutes for a message that never came.

I slam my palm against the marble tile, frustration bubbling up. "Fuck you, Vanessa." The words echo off the shower walls. A real friend would've shown up. A real friend wouldn't have left me vulnerable to Falchetti's calculated trap.

My fingers trace the bruises forming on my wrists from the zip ties. If Vanessa had been there watching my drinks, watching my back like she promised... I wouldn't be here now, wouldn't be a prisoner in this gilded cage.

Even Sofia's men failed me. I can still picture them huddled outside the club entrance, passing around cigarettes like teenage boys at recess. Amateur hour. All I had to do was slip through the back door while they were distracted. Some protection detail.

"We've got eyes on the little princess," I'd overheard one of them say into his phone earlier that night. The memory makes me want to scream. *Little princess? I showed them, didn't I?* Proved I could outsmart their pathetic surveillance.

A lot of good that did me. Now I'm trapped in the Falchetti's underground fortress, with that arrogant bastard playing prison guard. The same man who just stripped me bare without a second thought, like I was nothing more than a doll to be manhandled.

I press my forehead against the cool tile, letting the water drum against my back. The worst part? For a split second when his fingers grazed my skin, electricity shot through me. Heat that had nothing to do with anger or fear.

"Get it together, Elara," I mutter, scrubbing my skin raw as if I can wash away that moment of weakness. He's the enemy. The man who kidnapped me, who's using me as leverage against my family. Against Sofia.

But standing here in this luxurious shower, in this suite that feels more like a five-star hotel than a prison cell, confusion clouds my judgment. Why treat a hostage with such... consideration?

The Falchettis I grew up hearing about were monsters. Cold-blooded killers who'd stop at nothing to destroy anyone who crossed them. Not men who'd worry whether their captive had clean clothes or a comfortable bed.

I turn my face into the spray, letting it mask the tears I refuse to acknowledge. Everything I thought I knew about my world, about the players in this twisted game of power, seems to be unraveling.

Twenty-four hours ago, I was just Elara Moretti, the rebellious little sister trying to break free from Sofia's iron grip. Now I'm a pawn in a war I never asked to be part of, trapped between two families with decades of bad blood between them.

My fingers prune under the endless stream of hot water, but I can't bring myself to step out. Out there, a Falchetti waits. Out there, I have to face reality again. In here, I can pretend for just a few more minutes that this is all just a bad dream.

But the water can't wash away the truth. I'm alone in enemy territory, surrounded by people who see me as nothing more than collateral damage in their vendetta against my family. No friends to watch my back. No sister to protect me. Just me against the world.

"You still alive in there?" His deep voice carries through the door, playful despite our circumstances.

"Maybe I drowned." I call back, running my fingers through my wet hair. "Would that ruin your plans?"

"Entirely." A low chuckle follows. "Then I'd have to explain to the boss how I lost our leverage taking a shower."

"What a tragedy." I turn off the water, reaching for the plush white towel. "Though I suppose there are worse ways to go."

"Planning your escape through the drain pipes?"

"Please." I wrap the towel around myself, studying my reflection in the mirror. "I have standards. When I escape, it'll be much more dramatic."

His laugh sends an unexpected shiver down my spine. There's something magnetic about him, even through a closed door. Something that makes me forget, just for seconds at a time, that he's my captor.

I slip into the white robe hanging on the hook, soft cotton against my clean skin. My dark hair hangs wet down my back, dripping onto the marble floor as I pad toward the door.

When I step out, his eyes lock onto me. The playful banter dies in his throat. His gaze travels from my bare feet up to my face, lingering on the way the robe clings to my curves. The air between us crackles with electricity.

I shouldn't feel this pull toward him. He kidnapped me, for fuck's sake. But there's an intensity in his stare that makes my heart race. Makes me want to step closer, to see if he'd back away or draw me in.

"See something you like?" I tease, breaking the tension.

He clears his throat, but his eyes don't leave mine. "You clean up nice."

"For a hostage?"

"For anyone."

I move toward the bed, deliberately letting my hips sway. His sharp intake of breath is barely audible, but it sends a thrill through me. This is dangerous territory—playing with fire while surrounded by gasoline.

"You know," I say, perching on the edge of the mattress, "you haven't even told me your name—your *full* name. Seems only fair, since you know everything about me."

Something flickers across his face—hesitation, maybe guilt. He runs a hand through his dark hair, and for the first time, I see uncertainty in his stance.

"Luca," he says finally.

"Just Luca?"

"Luca Falchetti."

The air leaves my lungs in a rush. *Luca Falchetti.* Not just any soldier—he's one of them. My heart pounds against my ribs as pieces click into place. The authority in his stance, the way other men defer to him, how naturally he commands this space.

"You're…" I swallow hard. "You're not just working for them."

"No." His eyes hold mine, unflinching. "I'm not."

The revelation should terrify me. Should make me recoil, remember exactly who he is and what his family has done to mine. Instead, it adds another layer to the crackling tension between us.

"Were you ever going to tell me?" I ask, proud that my voice remains steady.

"Eventually." He takes a step closer, and I feel the heat radiating from his body. "When the time was right."

"And when would that be? After you got what you wanted?"

His lips curve into a dangerous smile. "What makes you think I know what I want?"

I rise from the bed, closing the distance between us until we're inches apart. "Because I see the way you look at me when you think I'm not watching."

"Dangerous game you're playing, Elara." His voice drops lower, sending shivers down my spine.

"I like dangerous." I tilt my chin up, meeting his gaze. "Or haven't you figured that out yet?"

His eyes darken as they drop to my lips. "I'm starting to."

I take another step closer, the cotton of my robe whispering against my skin. "You still haven't told me what you want, *Falchetti*." His name rolls off my tongue like honey laced with venom.

"Maybe I want to see how far you'll push this." His eyes track my movement as I circle him slowly, like a cat sizing up its prey. Though in this game, I'm not sure who's hunting whom.

"Afraid of what might happen if I do?" I trail my fingers across his shoulder blades, feeling the tension ripple through his muscles. The cotton of his shirt is soft beneath my touch.

He catches my wrist as I complete my circle, pulling me to face him. "I'm not afraid of anything, Elara."

"Liar." I twist my hand in his grip until our palms press together. "Everyone's afraid of something."

His thumb traces circles on my inner wrist, sending sparks of electricity up my arm. "What are you afraid of?"

"Right now?" I lean closer, close enough to catch the spicy notes of his cologne. "I'm afraid I might actually *like* you."

The Shower

A smile plays at the corners of his mouth. "That would be inconvenient."

"Tragic, really." I pull my hand free and step back, watching his eyes darken at the loss of contact. "What would Sofia say?"

"Let's not talk about your sister." He advances, matching my retreat step for step until my back hits the wall. "Not when there are so many more interesting topics."

"Like what?" I tilt my head, exposing the curve of my neck. His gaze follows the movement hungrily.

"Like why you keep playing with fire." He plants one hand on the wall beside my head, caging me in without touching. "You know who I am now. *What* I am."

"Maybe I like fire." I smooth an imaginary wrinkle from his shirt collar, letting my fingers brush against his throat. "Maybe I want to see if you burn as hot as they say."

His free hand captures mine, pressing it flat against his chest. Through the thin fabric, I feel his heart racing. "You're testing my control, little Moretti."

"Good." I curl my fingers, bunching his shirt in my fist. "I was starting to think you were made of ice."

He laughs, the sound rich and dark like aged whiskey. "Trust me, ice is the last thing on my mind right now."

"Prove it." The challenge slips out before I can stop it.

His eyes lock onto mine, searching for something. Weakness maybe, or fear. He won't find either. Whatever this is between us—attraction, manipulation, destiny—I'm all in.

"You don't know what you're asking for." His voice drops lower, sending shivers down my spine.

"I know exactly what I'm asking for." I release his shirt, smoothing the wrinkles I created. "Question is, are you man enough to give it to me?"

His jaw tightens. "I'm trying to protect you."

"From what? Yourself?" I arch an eyebrow. "Or are you protecting yourself from me?"

"Both." He pushes off the wall, creating space between us. The loss of his heat is almost physical. "This can't happen, Elara."

"Can't?" I follow him, refusing to let him retreat. "Or shouldn't?"

"Does it matter?"

"Everything matters." I press my palm against his cheek, feeling the scratch of stubble. "Every choice, every touch, every moment we pretend this isn't exactly what we both want."

His hand covers mine, but he doesn't pull it away. "Want isn't always enough."

"It could be." I rise on my tiptoes, bringing our faces level. "If you'd let it."

"You're impossible." The words come out as a growl.

"Part of my charm." I brush my thumb across his bottom lip. "Admit it, you like that about me."

His eyes flare with heat. "I like too many things about you. That's the problem."

"Only if you make it one." I drop my hand, taking a deliberate step back. "Ball's in your court, Falchetti. What are you going to do about it?"

equal upbringing
. . .

elara moretti

I lean against the plush velvet couch, pulling my knees to my chest as Luca settles beside me. The casino's muffled bass thrums through the walls, a distant heartbeat matching my own erratic pulse. His presence fills the space between us, electric and undeniable.

"What's it like in your family?" I ask, tracing the edge of my robe. "Growing up Falchetti?"

Luca's hazel eyes catch the dim light. "Probably not much different than being a Moretti. Always watching your back, learning who to trust." He runs a hand through his dark hair. "I was in law school when Dante needed me. Dropped everything to help him."

"You were going to be a lawyer?" The revelation surprises me. "That's... not what I expected."

"Yeah?" A ghost of a smile plays on his lips. "What did you expect? Some mindless thug who only knows how to break kneecaps?"

I can't help but laugh. "Maybe. Though you're definitely too pretty for that."

His eyes darken at my words, and heat crawls up my neck. "What about you?" he asks, voice low. "The artist in a family of killers?"

"Art was my escape." I twist a strand of damp hair around my finger. "Sofia tried to protect me from the worst of it, but... you can't really hide from what we are, can you?"

"No," he agrees softly. "It's in our blood."

"I lost my virginity at fifteen," I blurt out, not sure why I'm telling him this. "Started doing coke at sixteen. Like somehow that would make me belong more, you know? Make me harder."

Instead of judgment, I see understanding in his eyes. "We all try to prove ourselves. Different ways, same goal."

"Did it work for you? Giving up your dreams to be what they needed?"

Luca shifts closer, and I catch his scent—expensive cologne mixed with something uniquely him. "Sometimes I wonder. But family is everything, right? That's what they drill into us from birth."

"Family," I echo, tasting the bitterness of the word. "Even when they're the ones who hurt us most."

I shift on the couch, drawn closer to Luca like a magnet. Everything I've been taught screams that this is wrong - he's a Falchetti, the enemy. But looking at him now, seeing the depth in those hazel eyes, I can't bring myself to care.

"You're different than I imagined," I tell him, letting my hand rest inches from his on the velvet cushion. "Most men in our world, they're all sharp edges and ice. But you... there's something warm about you."

He raises an eyebrow. "Warm? That's not typically how people describe me."

"Then they're not paying attention." I lean in slightly, catching another whiff of his cologne. "You could've stayed on your path, become some hotshot lawyer. Instead, you chose family. That takes heart."

"Or stupidity," he counters, but I see the way his lips quirked up at the corners.

"Maybe both." I tuck my legs under me, angling my body toward his. "How old were you? When you left law school?"

"Twenty-four. Five years ago now."

Twenty-nine. The age gap should bother me—I'm barely eighteen—but it doesn't. If anything, his maturity, his understanding of both worlds, draws me in more.

"Do you regret it?" I press, genuinely curious. "Walking away from that life?"

His eyes meet mine, intense and searching. "Sometimes. But regret doesn't change anything. We make our choices and live with them."

"That's very philosophical of you, counselor." I flash him a teasing smile.

"Don't call me that." But there's no bite to his words.

"Why not? It suits you. The sharp mind behind that pretty face."

He shakes his head, but I catch the way his breath hitches slightly. "You're playing with fire, Elara."

"Maybe I like the heat." I lean closer still, until I can see the flecks of gold in his eyes. "Or maybe I'm tired of being the good little Moretti princess, locked away in her tower while everyone else lives."

"Is that what this is? Rebellion?"

"No." The word comes out softer than I intend. "This is... something else entirely."

His hand moves, fingers brushing against mine on the couch. Even that slight touch sends electricity racing up my arm. "We shouldn't."

"Another thing they drill into us from birth, right? All the things we shouldn't do." I turn my hand over, palm up - an invitation. "But you already broke their rules once, when you chose to help your cousin. How did that feel?"

"Like falling." His voice drops lower, sending shivers down my spine. "Like stepping off a cliff and trusting the ground would be there."

"And was it?"

"I survived the landing." His fingers trace patterns on my palm, each touch making my skin tingle. "But this... this is different."

"Because I'm a Moretti?"

"Because you're eighteen."

I can't help but roll my eyes. "I stopped being a child long ago. The moment I first saw someone die in our kitchen. The first time Sofia came home covered in blood. Age is just a number in our world - we grow up fast or we don't grow up at all."

His free hand comes up, tucking a strand of damp hair behind my ear. The gesture is so gentle it makes my heart ache. "You shouldn't have had to."

"But I did. We all did." I lean into his touch. "You understand that. You understand me."

"Elara..." My name on his lips sounds like a prayer and a warning all at once.

"Stop thinking so much, counselor." I slide closer, until our thighs touch. "For once in your life, just feel."

His eyes darken, and I see the internal war playing out behind them. The logical part of him - the lawyer, the strategist - fighting against whatever this magnetic pull is between us. I hold my breath, waiting to see which side wins.

His hand finds mine in the darkness, fingers intertwining. The touch sends sparks through my skin. "You're different than I expected, Moretti."

"Good different or bad different?"

"Dangerous different." His thumb traces circles on my palm. "You make me question things I shouldn't."

I turn to face him fully, my robe slipping slightly off one shoulder. "Like what?"

"Like whether doing my duty is worth losing something real." His free hand comes up to brush my cheek, and I lean into the touch. "You're supposed to be just another job."

"And you're supposed to be my captor." My heart pounds against my ribs. "We're both failing miserably at our roles."

His laugh is soft and warm. "Spectacularly."

We fall into comfortable silence, the weight of our shared understanding settling around us like a blanket. The casino's rhythm has changed to something slower, more sensual. It reminds me of countless nights spent in similar places, watching the dance between power and submission play out on the floor below.

"Sometimes I think about running away," I confess. "Just... disappearing. Becoming someone new."

"Where would you go?"

"Anywhere. Paris maybe. I could paint all day, live in a tiny apartment above a café." The fantasy feels real when I share it with him. "No family obligations, no blood feuds. Just art and coffee and freedom."

Luca's eyes hold mine, intense and searching. "Sounds lonely."

"Maybe." I bite my lip. "Unless I had the right company."

The air between us crackles with possibility. His gaze drops to my mouth, and I feel myself swaying toward him like a magnet finding true north.

A sudden chime from his watch makes us both jump. Luca glances at it, eyebrows rising. "It's two in the morning."

"What?" I grab his wrist to check for myself. "How did that happen?"

"Time flies when you're plotting escape routes with the enemy," he teases, but there's an edge of something real beneath the humor.

I realize we're still holding hands, neither of us willing to break the connection. "Are you really my enemy though?"

His expression softens into something that makes my chest ache. "No, Elara. I don't think I am anymore."

Luca's lips brush against mine, soft and insistent. It's a feather-light touch, yet it sends a jolt of electricity straight to my core. His hand slides around my waist, pulling me closer, and his tongue teases at the seam of my lips. I open for him, and our kiss deepens, tongues dancing in a slow, sensual tango. His kisses taste like sweet wine and dark chocolate, familiar but exotic, like nothing I've ever experienced.

His body presses against mine, and I can feel the heat emanating from his skin. I moan softly into his mouth as he grinds against me, and I arch into him, wanting more. My robe slips off one shoulder, revealing the curve of my breast. It's a small taste of freedom, and I shiver with anticipation.

Our lips part reluctantly, and he trails kisses down my jawline to my collarbone. I shudder as he nips at the soft skin, and a thrill of desire shoots straight to my crotch. His mouth grazes my robe, teasing me, and goosebumps rise on my skin. I can feel his erection pressing against my thigh, and I shimmy out of my robe in one smooth motion, letting it puddle around my ankles.

We're both naked now, our bodies glistening with sweat and desire. Luca's eyes rake over me, taking me in with an intensity that makes my toes curl. His hands glide up my thighs, and he cups my hips, pulling me onto him. My core instinctively searches for his, our aching need aligning perfectly.

"Elara," he murmurs, his voice rough with lust. "You're so beautiful. So damn beautiful."

Luca's palm cradles my breast, his thumb circling and teasing my nipple until it hardens into a tight peak. I arch my back, pressing myself into his touch, and a soft moan escapes my lips. His mouth trails a path of fire down my stomach, leaving a trail of goosebumps in its wake. He pauses at my hips, his fingers digging into my flesh as he looks up at me with hooded eyes. Then, his mouth is on me, his tongue flicking against my clit with expert precision. I gasp, my hips bucking against him, but he quickly pulls back, leaving me aching for more.

Luca's fingers slide down my body, finding my wetness and teasing my entrance. I moan, my body trembling with anticipation as he slowly pushes one finger inside me, then another. I rock against him, savoring the feeling of fullness as he curls his fingers, hitting that sweet spot that makes my toes curl.

"Luca," I gasp, my voice breathless with need. "Please, don't stop."

I feel him smile against my skin as he adds a third finger, stretching me wider. His thumb finds my clit again, rubbing slow circles as his fingers move in and out of me with excruciating slowness. I'm panting now, my hips moving in time with his rhythm, my body begging for release.

"You're so tight, Elara," Luca murmurs, his voice low and rough. "I can't wait to be inside you."

His words send a shiver down my spine, and I feel myself clench around his fingers. He groans, his own need evident in the strain of his voice.

"Please," I beg again, my voice barely above a whisper. "I need you … fuck me now."

He leans in to kiss me again, and I taste myself on his lips. It's intoxicating, addictive. Our hips move in sync, grinding against each other with a primal hunger. Every touch sends shockwaves through my body, every moan from him sends shivers down my spine.

I feel his thick erection brush against my entrance, and I gasp. He moves with deliberate slowness, pushing inside me inch by agonizing inch until he's fully seated. It's raw and intense and more than I've ever imagined. I bite my bottom lip to stifle a scream, feeling every sinew and muscle stretch to accommodate him.

He kisses my jaw, trails kisses down my neck, and nips gently at the lobe of my ear. "You feel so good," he murmurs. "So fucking good."

We start moving together, his hips undulating in a familiar rhythm. It's a perfect synchrony of our bodies, of our desires. His hands roam across my skin, his nails lightly scratching my back. I bite his shoulder, drawing blood, and he groans, pushing deeper into me.

The room spins around us—the dimmed lights, the smell of sweat and sex, the faint echo of the music from the casino below. It all blurs together as we lose ourselves in each other. Each thrust feels like a promise, each kiss a commitment. We're two people who shouldn't be here, shouldn't be doing this, but we can't seem to stop.

I wrap my legs around him, pulling him closer still. His skin slides against mine, silken and hot. Every thrust feels like a climax, and yet, I know this is just the beginning. Luca grips my hip, his nails digging in, and I bite my lip to stifle a cry of pleasure.

We find a pace that feels right, a rhythm that could go on forever. Heat pools between us, and sweat beads on our skin. Every touch sends shockwaves of ecstasy through me, and I cling to him, our hearts pounding in time.

And then, we're there. We climax together, our bodies shuddering with the force of it. Luca's grip tightens on me, pulling me closer still, and our mouths come together in unison, continuing to kiss and make out.

walk of shame

...

luca falchetti

My eyes flutter open to unfamiliar surroundings until recognition hits - the burgundy and gold wallpaper of the casino's private suite comes into focus. Reality crashes over me like ice water. I crossed a line I can't uncross.

Dante's face flashes in my mind, his stern expression when he ordered me to protect Elara. Not this. Never this. I run a hand over my face, mind racing to find a way to explain my actions to my cousin.

The weight of my responsibility presses down as I carefully extract myself from the tangled sheets. Elara sleeps peacefully beside me, dark hair fanned across the pillow, sheet draped low across her back. My hand hovers over her shoulder, drawn to the softness of her skin. I shouldn't.

But I do. I lean down and press a gentle kiss between her shoulder blades before forcing myself to step away. Duty calls.

I dress quickly and silently, my clothes from last night wrinkled but presentable enough. At the door, I pause for one last look at her sleeping form before slipping into the hallway.

Lorenzo stands at attention when I approach, his face carefully neutral. "I need you to watch her," I say, keeping my voice low. "She doesn't leave this room. Bring her whatever she needs - food, clothes, anything. But she stays put. Understood?"

He nods once, sharp and professional. "Yes, sir. No one in or out without your approval."

"Good." I straighten my jacket and head toward the main floor.

The disco lounge is a ghost of its nighttime self. Cleaning staff move methodically through the space, collecting empty glasses and wiping down surfaces. The pounding bass replaced by the quiet squeak of mops on the hardwood.

But the casino floor still pulses with energy, even at this hour. I weave between tables where bleary-eyed gamblers chase their losses or ride their winning streaks. A cheer erupts from the craps table as dice skitter across felt. The constant symphony of chips clicking, cards shuffling, and slot machines chiming fills the air.

I pause at the railing overlooking the high-stakes room. Below, serious faces hover over serious money. A player at the baccarat table pushes forward a stack of chips that could buy a car. The dealer's movements are precise, practiced. Money flows like water here, filling the family's coffers with each hand dealt.

My mind drifts back to Elara, to the warmth of her skin under my hands. I shake my head, trying to clear the memory. I'm supposed to be her protector, not her lover. But the damage is done. Now I just have to figure out how to face Dante and explain how I compromised everything for one night with the enemy's daughter.

The morning light streaming through high windows catches the gilded moldings, making them gleam. Another winner's shout echoes across the floor. Business as usual at the Falchetti casino, while upstairs my world has tilted on its axis.

I check my phone—no messages from Dante yet. Small mercies. But I know it's only a matter of time before I have to face him. Before I have to explain how I let desire override duty. How I put the family's plans at risk because I couldn't resist her.

The floor manager catches my eye, gesturing toward his office. Probably wants to review last night's take. I nod and start moving in his direction, grateful for the distraction of routine business. Anything to keep my mind off the girl sleeping in my bed upstairs and the storm that's surely coming when Dante finds out.

I follow Romeo into his office, grateful for the familiar routine of business. The morning light filters through the Venetian blinds, casting striped shadows across his meticulously organized desk.

"Numbers look strong," Romeo says, sliding a tablet across to me. His fingers tap efficiently through screens of data. "House is up twenty percent from last month."

I scan the figures, noting the steady climb in profits across all games. The poker tables have been particularly lucrative. "Impressive work. But we can do better."

Romeo raises an eyebrow, waiting for my direction. I've always appreciated his ability to read the room.

"Let's push it another ten percent," I say, leaning back in the leather chair. "Adjust the odds slightly on the high-stakes tables. Nothing obvious - we don't want to spook the whales."

He nods, already typing notes. "The regular players won't notice if we do it gradually. I'll have the dealers implement the changes over the next few shifts."

"Good." I stand and straighten my jacket. "Make sure the staff understands discretion is paramount. We don't need any loose lips about house advantages."

"Of course, Mr. Falchetti." Romeo rises as well, smoothing his perfectly pressed shirt. "I'll brief the floor supervisors personally. They'll handle the individual dealer instructions."

Through the office window, I watch as he steps onto the casino floor, gathering his team for a huddle. Their faces are serious, professional - exactly what we need. Romeo runs a tight ship, which is why Giovanni trusts him with this operation.

The thought of Giovanni reminds me of the impending conversation with Dante. But for now, I focus on the business at hand. The casino is one of our most profitable ventures, laundering money through a steady stream of legitimate gambling losses. The cleaner the operation looks, the better for everyone.

I move to the window, observing the early morning crowd. A woman in sequins celebrates at the roulette table, clearly riding last night's winning streak into the dawn. An elderly man methodically feeds coins into his favorite slot machine, lost in the hypnotic rhythm of spinning reels.

Romeo returns, tablet in hand. "All set, sir. I've instructed the supervisors to implement the changes gradually over the next three shifts. They'll monitor player reactions and adjust accordingly."

"Perfect." I clap him on the shoulder. "Giovanni and Dante will be pleased with these numbers. Keep up the good work."

His chest puffs slightly at the praise. Everyone knows Giovanni's approval is gold in our world. "Thank you, Mr. Falchetti. Will you be staying to observe the morning shift change?"

"No, I have other matters to attend to." My thoughts drift upstairs again, but I push them away. "Send me the daily reports as usual."

I exit his office, noting how the staff straightens imperceptibly as I pass. The Falchetti name carries weight and demands respect. It's something I've grown used to over the years, though it still feels strange sometimes - this power that comes with the family legacy.

The morning crowd is starting to thin, replaced by the early birds hoping to catch the looser machines. A cocktail waitress weaves between tables with coffee instead of martinis. The shift change brings a fresh energy to the floor, dealers counting in and out while supervisors watch with sharp eyes.

Romeo's team is already implementing the new protocols. I catch subtle adjustments in dealing patterns, slightly modified shuffle sequences. Nothing that would raise suspicion among the players, but enough to edge the house advantage up that crucial percentage.

This is what we do best - work the margins, control the flow of money and power with such precision that no one sees the puppet strings. It's a delicate dance, one that requires constant vigilance and adjustment.

The familiar rhythm of chips clicking and cards shuffling follows me as I cross the floor. It's almost meditative, this constant soundtrack of fortune-changing hands. Most of it flows our way, of course - that's just good business.

A supervisor catches my eye and nods, confirming the new instructions are being followed. I return the gesture, satisfied with the smooth operation of our family's crown jewel. The casino represents everything the Falchetti name stands for - power, precision, and profitability wrapped in a veneer of legitimate entertainment.

I check my phone again - still no word from Dante. The morning stretches ahead, full of potential complications. But for now, at least this part of our empire runs like clockwork, generating the steady stream of clean money that keeps our other ventures funded and our influence growing.

"Mr. Falchetti!" Marco's voice cuts through my thoughts as he hurries across the casino floor, dodging between early-morning players. His usually composed face is tight with concern. "Where have you been? We've been trying to reach you."

I wave him off, not wanting to discuss my whereabouts. "Just handling some business. What's so urgent?"

"It's Dante, sir." Marco lowers his voice, glancing around at nearby tables. "He was shot last night during the raid. They rushed him to the mansion. The doctor's been with him for hours."

The words hit me like a physical blow. Shot? My hand instinctively reaches for my phone - no messages, no missed calls. *How did I miss this?*

"When?" I demand, grabbing Marco's arm. "When did this happen?"

"Around midnight, from what I heard. Sofia Moretti's men ambushed them at the warehouse." Marco's words fade as blood rushes in my ears.

Walk of Shame

Midnight. While I was upstairs with Elara, lost in pleasure, my cousin was bleeding out across town. Bile rises in my throat.

"I have to go." I cut Marco off mid-sentence, already moving toward the exit. My footsteps echo across the marble floor as I break into a run.

The morning sun blinds me as I burst out of the casino's side entrance. My hands shake as I fumble with my car keys, missing the lock twice before managing to wrench the door open.

The engine roars to life and I peel out of the parking lot, tires squealing against asphalt. My knuckles turn white on the steering wheel as I weave through traffic, ignoring horns and angry shouts.

Dante shot. The words keep pounding in my head with each heartbeat. My cousin, my blood, fighting for his life while I was...

Shame burns hot in my chest. I should have been there. Should have had his back like always. Instead, I was between the sheets with Elara Moretti - the enemy's daughter. The very person we're supposed to be using as leverage.

I slam my palm against the steering wheel. "Fuck!" The word explodes from my throat, raw with self-loathing. Some protector I turned out to be - betraying both my assignments in one night.

The mansion appears ahead, its stone facade stern and accusatory in the morning light. Security waves me through without stopping - they know my car, know my face. Know I belong here.

But do I? After what I've done?

I screech to a stop in front of the main entrance, leaving the car running as I leap out. My feet carry me up the familiar steps two at a time, each second heavy with the weight of my disloyalty.

The grand foyer stretches before me, usually a symbol of Falchetti power and tradition. Today it feels like a gauntlet I have to run, each step bringing me closer to facing the consequences of my actions.

Giovanni's words echo in my memory: "Family first. Always." It was his most important lesson, drilled into us since childhood. And I failed. Failed Dante, failed the family, failed everything we stand for.

Guards and staff move quickly out of my way as I stride through the mansion's corridors. They must see something in my face - urgency, guilt, fear. I don't care. All that matters is getting to Dante.

The thick carpet muffles my footsteps as I approach his wing of the house. More guards here, faces grim and watchful. They nod as I pass, unaware of my betrayal. Unaware that while they were protecting our family, I was compromising everything for a moment of weakness.

My heart pounds against my ribs as I near Dante's rooms. Through the heavy wooden doors, I can hear muffled voices - the doctor giving instructions, someone responding in low tones. Lila's voice, I think, though I can't make out the words.

the café

. . .

dante falchetti

Through the haze of pain, I hear Luca's rushed footsteps entering the room. His face appears above me, twisted with concern and guilt as he takes in the sight of the doctor working on my wounds.

"I should've been there," Luca says, his voice tight. "This is my fault."

I shake my head, fighting to keep my voice steady despite the burning in my side. "You were exactly where you needed to be. Protecting our asset." I fix him with a hard stare. "Is she safe?"

Luca's shoulders slump slightly. "Yes. She's secure in the casino suites."

"Good." I try to sit up, but Lila's hand on my shoulder keeps me down. The doctor shoots me a warning look. "I have a plan to get Enzo and Mia back. We're going to hit Sofia where it hurts."

"You can barely move," Lila protests, her fingers tightening on my shoulder. "This is insane."

"My brother's out there." I cover her hand with mine. "I won't leave him at Sofia's mercy."

Luca steps closer, his expression thoughtful. "What's the plan?"

"I'm going to contact Sofia. Set up a meet." I grimace as the doctor finishes bandaging my side. "A trade—Elara for Enzo."

Lila's face pales. "You can't trust her."

"I don't." I reach for my phone, typing out a message to Sofia. Within minutes, it buzzes with her response.

Luca reads the message over my shoulder and frowns. "A public cafe? And she wants you to come alone? This has *trap* written all over it."

"Which is exactly why it'll work." I push myself to sitting position, ignoring the protest of my wounds. "She'll be expecting a trap. She won't see the real one coming."

"I don't like this," Lila says, but I can see the resignation in her eyes. She knows she can't stop me.

"You don't have to." I stand slowly, testing my balance. "But I'm doing it anyway."

I lean back against the leather headrest, memories flooding in despite my efforts to stay focused on the present threat. Sofia's face swims before my eyes - not the hard, vengeful mask she wears now, but how she looked before. Before everything went to hell.

The last time I saw her, she had Lila bound to a chair in that abandoned warehouse. The pure hatred in Sofia's eyes as she

The Café

pressed the gun to Lila's temple still haunts me. "I want my money," she had snarled.

My jaw clenches at the memory. If I had been even a minute later... I shake my head, pushing the thought away. Lila survived. That's what matters.

But Sofia wasn't always capable of such cruelty. Years ago, when we were younger, she had a softness to her that few got to see. Behind closed doors, away from the weight of our families' expectations, I saw glimpses of the real Sofia - passionate, fierce in her loyalty, but with a gentleness that surprised me. The way she'd laugh, *really* laugh, head thrown back and guard completely down. How she'd curl into my side late at night, whispering her dreams of changing things, making the family legitimate.

I remember the exact moment it all changed. The day they buried her father, Sofia stood like a statue at the graveside. When everyone else had gone, she remained, and I stayed with her. She didn't cry - Sofia never cried. But something in her eyes died that day. The crown of the Moretti family settled on her head like a curse, transforming her into something hard and cruel.

"Power reveals who we truly are," she told me later that night. "And I'm done being weak."

A sharp pain in my side pulls me from the memories. Gritting my teeth, I push myself to a standing position. The doctor's handiwork holds, but barely. Each movement sends fresh waves of agony through my torso.

Still, I force myself to walk. One foot in front of the other. The pain grounds me in reality, reminds me what's at stake. Enzo's life hangs in the balance. Mia's too. I can't afford to let old feelings cloud my judgment.

My reflection in the window shows a man ready for war, despite the bandages hidden beneath my shirt. Good. Sofia needs to see strength when we meet. Any hint of weakness and she'll pounce - that's who she is now. The woman I once loved is gone, replaced by someone who would burn the world down just to watch me suffer in the flames.

I reach the end of the room and turn, pacing back. Each step becomes easier, my body adjusting to movement. The pain fades to a dull throb, manageable. I've worked through worse.

"You should be resting," Lila says from the doorway, concern etched on her face.

"Can't afford to rest." I continue my measured pace. "Sofia's expecting the injured lion. She'll be watching for signs of weakness. I need to show her I'm still dangerous."

"You are dangerous," Lila replies softly. "But you're also human. Don't push too hard."

I pause, looking at her. The worry in her eyes reminds me why I can't fail. Sofia tried to take this from me once. She failed then, and she'll fail now. I won't let her destroy anything else I love.

My phone buzzes again - another message from Sofia. The cafe meeting is set for noon tomorrow. Sixteen hours to prepare, to get my body ready for whatever she has planned. Sixteen hours to ensure my trap is perfect.

I resume my pacing, each step more determined than the last. The pain sharpens my focus, clears my mind of old memories and might-have-beens. Sofia made her choice long ago. Tomorrow, she'll learn the cost of targeting my family.

* * *

The Café

I ADJUST MY SUIT JACKET, ignoring the burning protest from my side as I settle into the back of the black SUV. Through the tinted windows, the city lights blur past, each flash a reminder of the empire I've helped build. The weight of command sits heavy on my shoulders tonight.

"Everything's in position, sir," Marco reports from the driver's seat. "Teams are stationed around the warehouse perimeter. They await your signal."

I nod, checking my phone one last time. The tracking data shows movement inside the warehouse - multiple heat signatures. Enzo has to be in there. My brother, always the wild card, now caught in Sofia's web of vengeance.

"Remember the priority," I tell Marco. "Get Enzo out first. Whatever it takes."

The car glides through the empty streets as we head toward the cafe. My mind drifts to the day Father named me his second in command. I was twenty-two, fresh blood still drying on my hands from my first hit. The pride in his eyes mixed with something darker - expectation. The crown of responsibility settled onto my head that day, each jewel a different burden to bear.

"Sir?" Marco's voice pulls me back. "We're five minutes out from the cafe."

I straighten, pushing aside memories of the past. The present demands my full attention. "Status update on the warehouse team?"

"In position. Waiting on your command."

My phone vibrates - a message from Giovanni.

> Remember who we are

As if I could forget. The Falchetti name is carved into my bones, written in the blood I've spilled and the sacrifices I've made.

The cafe comes into view, its cheerful facade a stark contrast to the darkness of our world. Sofia chose well - public enough to discourage outright violence, private enough for whatever game she plans to play.

"Circle the block," I instruct Marco. "I want one more look at the approaches."

The streets around the cafe are quiet, but my trained eye catches the subtle signs - a car parked at an odd angle, a "maintenance" van that's been there too long. Sofia's people, no doubt. She's as thorough as ever.

I check my watch. Ten minutes until the meeting. Time to set everything in motion.

"Give the warehouse team the green light," I tell Marco. "Full force. No hesitation."

He relays the order through a secure channel while I prepare myself for what's to come. The gun at my hip is a familiar comfort, though I doubt I'll need it. This meeting isn't about firepower - it's about control. About showing Sofia that targeting my family was her biggest mistake.

The car completes its circuit and pulls up to the cafe. Through the window, I can see Sofia already inside, sitting at a corner table. She's alone, as agreed, but I know her backup is close. Just like mine.

"Sir," Marco says quietly. "Are you sure about this?"

I meet his eyes in the rearview mirror. "No choice. Family first. Always."

The Café

The words taste bitter on my tongue, memories of Sofia threatening to surface again. We were family once too, in a way. Before ambition and revenge poisoned everything between us.

My phone buzzes again - the warehouse team is in position. Everything hinges on perfect timing now. While Sofia's attention is focused on me, my men will strike. A classic diversion, but sometimes the old plays work best.

I adjust my cuffs, a habit born from years of preparing for confrontation. The bandages under my shirt pull tight, a sharp reminder of recent violence. But pain is an old friend by now. I've learned to use it, to let it sharpen my focus rather than dull it.

"If anything goes wrong," I tell Marco, "get word to Giovanni immediately. He'll know what to do."

Marco nods, his hand resting on his own weapon. "Good luck, sir."

I step out of the car, the cool air hitting my face. Each step toward the cafe door feels weighted with purpose. This isn't just about Enzo anymore. It's about sending a message. The Falchetti family protects its own, no matter the cost.

Through the glass, Sofia watches me approach. Her face is a mask of calm, but I know her tells. The slight tension in her shoulders, the way her fingers tap against her coffee cup - she's nervous. Good. She should be.

I pause at the door, hand on the handle. In my ear, the comm unit crackles softly. The warehouse team is ready. Everything is in place.

I take a deep breath, letting the familiar mantle of authority settle over me. Time to play my part in this dangerous game.

I'm sliding into a chair across from Sofia—she looks exactly as I remember—beautiful and deadly, like a poisonous flower. Her dark eyes watch me carefully as I settle in, noting every wince of pain.

"You're looking rough, Dante," she says, stirring her untouched coffee. "Getting sloppy in your old age?"

"Let's skip the small talk." I lean forward, keeping my voice low. "I'm here to make a deal. Elara for Enzo. Clean trade, no tricks."

Sofia's mask slips for just a moment, and I catch a glimpse of the woman I used to know. The one who dreamed of a different life, before power and revenge consumed her. "You know I can't do that."

"Can't? Or won't?" I hold her gaze. "This ends now, Sofia. Before more blood is spilled."

"It's not that simple." Her fingers tremble slightly as she reaches for her cup. "It was never that simple with us, was it?"

I study Sofia's face, searching for any sign of deception. But all I see is that familiar longing in her eyes - the same look she used to give me years ago when we'd talk about our future together. Might as well play along if it keeps her distracted.

"We had plans once," I say carefully, watching her reaction. "Before everything went sideways."

"We were unstoppable." Sofia's voice softens with nostalgia. "The Falchetti and Moretti families united. Can you imagine what we could have built together?"

"I remember." And I do - late nights planning empire expansions, discussing mergers over expensive wine, her brilliant mind working in sync with mine. Before the betrayals. Before the blood. "You always did think big."

The Café

"Because I knew what we were capable of." She reaches across the table, her fingers stopping just short of touching mine. "We could have ruled this city, Dante. Your strength, my cunning. No one could have stood against us."

I force myself to stay still, fighting the urge to pull away. "That was a different time. Different people."

"Are we really so different?" Sofia's dark eyes search mine. "I still think about you. About us. Every major decision, every move I make - I wonder what you would think, what you would say."

The confession hits harder than I expect. I remember how in sync we were, how she used to read my thoughts before I voiced them. "Sofia—"

"Don't." She cuts me off, pain flashing across her face. "Don't say it doesn't matter anymore. It matters. It's always mattered." Her voice drops to barely above a whisper. "Even after everything, I've never stopped caring about what you think of me."

I think of Lila waiting at home, of Enzo held captive somewhere in this twisted game. But part of me - the part I try to bury - understands exactly what Sofia means. We were forged in the same fire, shaped by the same brutal world.

"We could have been legendary," she continues, a familiar passion lighting her eyes. "The perfect merger of our families' strengths. Your tactical mind, my business sense. Together, we could have transformed everything."

"Into what?" I ask, genuinely curious despite myself. "What did you imagine for us?"

"Legitimacy." Sofia leans forward, her coffee forgotten. "Real power, not just street control. Political connections, clean businesses. A legacy our children could inherit without shame."

The mention of children sends an unexpected pang through my chest. Another dream lost to violence and betrayal. "You really thought that far ahead?"

"Of course I did." Her smile is bitter-sweet. "I planned everything - where we'd live, how we'd raise our family, how we'd slowly transition the business. I even had names picked out."

I remember finding her notebook once, filled with careful plans and dreams. Pages of potential business ventures, sketches of house layouts, even a family tree with our imagined children's names. I'd teased her about it then, but secretly, I'd been touched by how much thought she'd put into our future.

"That future died with your father," I say quietly.

"Did it have to?" Her hand inches closer to mine. "We could still—"

"Don't." Now it's my turn to cut her off. "You know we can't go back."

"But we could go forward." Sofia's voice takes on an urgent edge. "Think about it, Dante. All these years of fighting, and for what? We could still build something together. Different from what we planned, but still ours."

I feel the weight of history between us, years of shared dreams and spilled blood. Every choice that led us here, every betrayal and missed opportunity. Part of me wants to believe her - the young man who once thought we could conquer the world together.

"The things we've done to each other," I say carefully, "they can't be undone."

"No," she agrees. "But they could be understood. Forgiven, maybe. We're the only ones who truly know each other, Dante.

The Café

The only ones who understand what it means to carry these names, these responsibilities."

Her words echo my own thoughts from darker moments, and I hate how well she still knows me. How easily she can reach past my defenses and touch the parts of me I try to keep buried.

"I've missed this," she admits softly. "Just talking with you. Being understood without having to explain myself. No one else has ever known me like you do."

"Sofia—"

"I wanted to be yours," she blurts out, her composure cracking. "A Falchetti. Your wife. That's all I ever wanted." Her laugh is bitter. "Stupid girl's dreams, right?"

I sit back, the weight of her words settling between us like lead. The Sofia I knew is still in there somewhere, buried beneath layers of hate and ambition. But I can't reach her anymore. That bridge burned long ago.

"The past is the past," I say quietly. "This is about now. About Enzo and Elara."

Her face hardens, walls slamming back into place. After a long pause, she shakes her head. "No deal."

escape the warehouse
...

enzo falchetti

My wrists burn from the constant friction of ropes and chains, muscles aching from being tied to this damn chair for what feels like forever. Beside me, Mia's eyes are red from crying, but her spirit hasn't broken. We've tried escaping three times now, each attempt ending with rougher treatment from Sofia's men.

The ropes dig deeper into my wrists as I shift again, trying to find any position that might ease the burning sensation. My shoulders scream in protest from being locked in place for days. The metallic taste of dried blood lingers on my split lip, a constant reminder of our failed escape attempts.

"Stay still," I whisper to Mia when she starts fidgeting beside me. "Save your strength." My heart twists seeing her like this – exhausted, disheveled, with dark circles under her eyes. This is my fault. If I'd been more careful, if I'd seen through Sofia's trap...

Where the hell is everyone? Father should have made a move by now. And Dante – my brother never leaves loose ends hanging. Something must be holding them back, some angle I'm not seeing. *Sofia's playing a bigger game here, but what?*

I scan the dim warehouse for the hundredth time, mapping every shadow, every potential exit. The guards rotate shifts every six hours. They're professionals, never dropping their guard, never giving us an opening. But Sofia herself hasn't shown her face in days. Just her thugs, bringing stale bread and water, checking our restraints with rough hands.

My muscles cramp again and I grit my teeth against the pain. The dried blood on my face itches like crazy, flaking off whenever I move. My clothes are stiff with sweat and grime. I can't remember the last time I felt this disgusting, this helpless.

"I need to get you out of here," I mutter, more to myself than Mia. She looks up at me with those determined eyes, still showing fire despite everything. But I see how the captivity is wearing her down – her usually bright face dulled by exhaustion and fear.

The warehouse creaks and groans around us, the sounds amplified by our heightened senses. Every footstep could be Sofia returning. Every distant car engine could be rescue arriving. The waiting is the worst part – not knowing what's coming next, what game Sofia's playing with my family.

I flex my fingers, trying to maintain circulation despite the tight bonds. *Think, Enzo. There has to be something I'm missing.* Sofia's too smart to just leave us here without a purpose. She wants something specific, something worth risking the full wrath of the Falchetti family.

A rat scurries across the floor nearby, and Mia jumps slightly. I wish I could reach out and comfort her, tell her everything will be okay. But we both know better than to make promises we can't keep. The truth is, we're running out of time and options.

The guard by the door shifts his weight, checking his watch. Almost time for the next rotation. I've memorized their patterns, their habits. Not that it helps much when you're tied to a chair, but information is power in our world. Any detail could be the key to survival.

My head throbs from dehydration and lack of sleep. *How long has it been since we've had more than a few sips of water?* The hunger I can handle – growing up Falchetti teaches you to endure discomfort – but watching Mia suffer through it tears me apart.

"When we get out of here," I say quietly, keeping my voice low enough that the guards won't hear, "I'm taking you somewhere safe. Somewhere far from all this." She gives me a weak smile, but we both know it's an empty promise. There's no escaping this life, not really. Not for me, and now, because of me, not for her either.

Another engine rumbles in the distance, and I hold my breath, listening. It fades away like all the others. Not rescue. Not Sofia. Not anything that could end this nightmare. Just another false hope in an endless string of disappointments.

The guard's radio crackles with static, making us both flinch. But it's just a routine check-in, nothing useful. I strain my ears, trying to pick up any information from their mumbled conversations. They're careful though, professional. Sofia chose her men well.

A drop of sweat rolls down my back, making me even more aware of how filthy I feel. My muscles ache for movement, for a hot shower, for any kind of relief from this forced stillness. But more than my own discomfort, I hate seeing Mia reduced to this state. She deserves better than being caught in the crossfire of Falchetti-Moretti politics.

"Keep still," I whisper to Mia as footsteps echo outside again. "Maybe they'll—"

Gunfire erupts outside, sharp cracks splitting the air. Mia flinches beside me.

"Get down!" I strain against my chains. "Keep your head low, baby."

The warehouse door crashes open. My heart pounds as boots thunder across concrete. But instead of Sofia's thugs, I see familiar faces – *our* guys, *our* colors. And then—

"Luca!" Relief floods through me at the sight of my cousin, tactical vest over his suit, gun drawn.

"Clear the room!" Luca barks orders to our men before rushing over. "You okay, cuz?"

"Been better." I manage a weak laugh as one of the guys starts cutting through my chains. "But alive."

"Get the girl free too," Luca commands, helping me to my feet as I'm released. My legs shake, but I pull him into a fierce hug.

"Thought you forgot about us," I mumble into his shoulder.

"Never." He squeezes back. "Family first, always."

My legs still feel weak as I lean against Luca, memories flooding back as the adrenaline starts to fade. The familiar scent of his cologne – that expensive stuff he always wears – brings back a rush of memories from simpler times.

"Remember those nights at *Club Azure*?" I can't help but grin despite my exhaustion. "Back when Dante got promoted to second?"

Luca's eyes light up with recognition. "How could I forget? Your brother strutted around like he owned the place."

"He practically did." I laugh, wincing at the pain in my ribs. "Dad had just given him the keys to the kingdom, and man, did he know how to work it."

"Come here, baby," I coherce Mia as she melts under my shoulder. I hold her tight and she holds me even tighter.

The warehouse buzzes with activity as our men secure the perimeter, but my mind drifts to those golden days. Dante, always in his perfectly tailored suits, commanding attention without saying a word. The way the crowds would part for him, like Moses and the Red Sea. And Luca, with that easy charm of his, drawing people in with just a smile.

"You two were impossible to keep up with," I tell him, shaking my head. "Every time I turned around, there'd be another group of admirers hanging on your every word."

"You did alright for yourself, little cousin." Luca helps me stay steady as we walk toward the exit. "As I recall, you never went home alone."

"Only because you two left your leftovers." But there's no bitterness in my voice – just fondness for those carefree nights when our biggest worry was which club to hit next. Mia gives me a pinch.

God, we were unstoppable back then. Dante fresh in his power, Luca already establishing himself as the family's sharpest mind, and me... well, I was just happy to be part of it all. The legendary Falchetti boys, turning heads and breaking hearts across the city.

"You remember that night Dante cleared out the VIP section just because some guy looked at him wrong?" I ask, grateful for the distraction from my aching body.

"And ended up buying drinks for the whole club to smooth it

over?" Luca chuckles. "Classic Dante. All fire and fury one minute, charm and generosity the next."

Looking at Luca now, still every bit the collected professional even in tactical gear, it's hard to reconcile him with the wild card he used to be. We've all changed, grown into our roles in the family. But underneath it all, we're still those three kids who'd tear up the town together.

"I always wanted to be like you two," I admit, the words slipping out before I can stop them. Maybe it's the exhaustion talking. "You and Dante, you always seemed to know exactly who you were, what you wanted."

Luca's grip on my arm tightens slightly. "We were just better at faking it, cuz. Trust me."

My eyes drift to where our men are helping Mia now toward a waiting car. Even beaten down and exhausted, she's the most beautiful thing I've ever seen. "Guess some things work out the way they're supposed to, though."

"Speaking of which," Luca's voice turns serious, "we need to get you both checked out. Medical team's standing by."

I nod, but my mind's still dancing through memories of those golden days. The three of us, young and invincible, ruling our little corner of the world. Dante with his intensity, Luca with his wit, and me... always watching, always learning from them both.

Nothing meant more than family back then. Still doesn't, if I'm being honest. Well, almost nothing – my eyes find Mia again, and my heart clenches. Family's everything, but she's become part of that everything now, woven into the fabric of my life as surely as Dante and Luca.

"You good to walk?" Luca asks, pulling me from my thoughts.

"Yeah," I straighten up, finding my strength. "Just... thanks, Luca. For coming for us. For always having my back, like the old days."

He gives me that familiar half-smile, the one that used to make hearts flutter across every dance floor in the city. "Always will, little cousin. That's what family's for."

The drive back to the estate passes in a blur of exhaustion and relief. Mia stays pressed against my side, her hand clutched in mine. When we arrive, Dad's waiting in the foyer.

"Son." His voice cracks as he embraces me. It's rare to see Giovanni Falchetti show emotion, but today his eyes are damp.

"I'm okay, Papa." I hold him tight, breathing in the familiar scent of his cologne.

Heavy footsteps announce another arrival. I turn to see Dante striding in, Lila at his side. My big brother's face breaks into an uncharacteristic grin.

"Little brother." He wraps me in a bear hug that nearly lifts me off my feet. "Don't ever scare me like that again."

"No promises." I laugh, wincing as he jostles my bruised ribs.

"We've got leverage now," Dante says, expression turning serious. "Grabbed Elara Moretti. She's secure at the casino."

Luca nods. "Just checked on her. She's safe, contained."

I take a deep breath, squeezing Mia's hand. "Speaking of family matters..." All eyes turn to me. "I've asked Mia to marry me."

The room erupts in congratulations. Papa claps me on the back, pride shining in his eyes. Dante pulls both Mia and me into another hug.

"About time," Luca says with a smirk.

"Well..." Dante clears his throat. "Since we're sharing news..." He pulls Lila closer. "I've asked this beautiful woman to be my wife."

Lila beams, stretching up to kiss him. "And I said yes." She pauses, a familiar gleam entering her eye – the one that usually means trouble.

I lean back, watching my family celebrate around me. Despite everything we've been through, despite Sofia's threats still hanging over us, in this moment we're just family – damaged and dangerous, but family all the same.

the treaty

...

dante falchetti

I lean back in my leather chair, watching Lila pace the study. The late afternoon sun casts long shadows across the hardwood floor, matching my dark thoughts. My side still aches from the bullet wound, a constant reminder of how close we came to disaster.

"Sofia will never stop, will she?" Lila's voice breaks through my brooding.

"No." I run a hand over my face, exhaustion seeping into my bones. "She's like a force of nature – unstoppable once she sets her mind to something."

Lila stops pacing, her green eyes fixing on me with that penetrating gaze I've come to both love and fear. "What does she really want, Dante? Beyond the power plays and the violence?"

"Me." The word tastes bitter on my tongue. "She wants to marry me, to become a Falchetti. It's always been her endgame."

I watch Lila's mouth snap shut, her lips pressing into a thin line. The silence stretches between us like a physical thing, heavy and suffocating. My chest tightens at her reaction, but I force myself to stay still, to give her the space to process what I've just revealed.

The sunlight catches in her fiery red hair, creating a halo effect that makes my heart ache. Even in moments like these, her beauty strikes me with devastating force. But it's not just her looks that drew me in – it's her strength, her fierce spirit that refuses to break no matter what life throws at her.

I search her face for signs of hurt, of betrayal, but find only that steely determination I've come to know so well. Relief washes over me. Lila isn't some delicate flower that wilts at the first sign of trouble. She's weathered worse storms than this revelation about Sofia's obsession with me.

"When?" The single word cuts through the silence, sharp as a blade.

"It started years ago, before I met you." I lean forward, ignoring the protest from my wounded side. "Sofia and I... there was something between us once. But it was never what she wanted it to be."

Lila's eyes narrow slightly. "And what did she want it to be?"

"A fairytale. The perfect mafia marriage – joining two powerful families through their heirs." I can't keep the bitterness from my voice. "But I saw through her act. Everything was calculated, every move designed to get her closer to power. There was nothing real about it."

"Unlike us?" There's a challenge in her tone now.

"Christ, Lila." I push myself up from the chair, crossing the space between us despite the pain. "What we have – it's the realest thing in my life. That's why I'm telling you this. No secrets, no lies, no carefully crafted stories to protect your feelings."

She doesn't back away as I approach, standing her ground like always. "Because you think I can handle it?"

"Because I know you can." I reach for her hand, relief flooding through me when she doesn't pull away. "And because I love you too damn much to build our future on anything less than complete honesty."

The tension in her shoulders eases slightly, but her grip on my hand is fierce. "Tell me everything, then. I want to know exactly what we're dealing with."

I trace my thumb over her knuckles, gathering my thoughts. "Sofia's dangerous not just because she's ruthless, but because she truly believes she deserves this – deserves me, deserves to be a Falchetti. In her mind, you're the obstacle standing between her and her destiny."

"She's delusional," Lila scoffs.

"She's desperate," I correct her. "And desperate people are unpredictable. That's why I needed you to know. Every move she makes from here on out will be calculated to hurt you, to drive a wedge between us."

Lila steps closer, her free hand coming up to rest against my chest, right over my heart. "Then she doesn't know us very well, does she?"

The fierce pride that swells in my chest almost overwhelms me. This woman – this incredible, fearless woman – stands before the threat of a vengeful mafia princess without flinching. She deserves nothing less than my complete trust, my absolute honesty.

"No, she doesn't." I cup her face in my hands, studying the determination blazing in those green eyes. "Sofia thinks love is a weakness she can exploit. She doesn't understand that what we have makes us stronger."

"Good." Lila's lips curve into a dangerous smile. "Let her underestimate us. It'll be her biggest mistake."

My thumb traces the line of her jaw as something dark and possessive coils in my gut. The truth might hurt, might expose old wounds and uncomfortable realities, but Lila takes it all in stride. She doesn't shy away from the ugliness of my world or the dangers that come with loving me.

"Marrying you is never going to happen." Lila's voice carries steel beneath the velvet. She moves closer, perching on the edge of my desk. "But what if we could give her something else? *Someone* else?"

I raise an eyebrow. "What are you suggesting?"

"In medieval times, powerful families would arrange marriages to forge peace treaties, to stop wars between nations." Her eyes sparkle with intelligence. "Political alliances through marriage—it's an ancient solution to a modern problem."

The idea starts taking root in my mind. "A marriage alliance between the Falchetti and Moretti families?" I lean forward, intrigued despite myself. "It's an interesting thought, but who? Enzo's spoken for now."

"What about Luca?"

The suggestion hits me like a thunderbolt. I stand, ignoring the protest from my wound, and walk to the window. "Luca and Sofia?" The pieces start falling into place in my mind. "He's my cousin, a true Falchetti. It could work."

"It would give her what she wants – the Falchetti name – and potentially end this bloodshed."

I turn back to Lila, marveling at her strategic mind. "Get Luca in here. Now."

MINUTES LATER, Luca stands before my desk, his expression guarded. I can see the weight of recent events in the shadows under his eyes.

"I have a proposition for you," I begin, measuring my words carefully. "Sofia Moretti has made it clear she wants to be a Falchetti. We can use that to our advantage, to forge a peace between our families."

Luca's jaw tightens. "What are you asking?"

"I'm asking you to marry Sofia Moretti." The words hang heavy in the air between us. "Create an alliance that could end this war once and for all."

I watch the emotions play across his face – shock, confusion, resignation. Finally, he squares his shoulders. "If this is what it takes to make things right, to protect our family..." He pauses, and I can see the internal struggle. "I'll do it. I'll marry Sofia."

The weight of his sacrifice isn't lost on me. I stand and place a hand on his shoulder. "Thank you, cousin. This could change everything."

Luca nods, his expression hardening into resolve. "When do we make the offer?"

"Soon. We need to move quickly while the opportunity is fresh." I look between him and Lila. "This could be our chance to finally bring peace to both families."

***

luca falchetti

The porcelain feels cool against my forehead as I heave into the toilet, my stomach twisting with each wave of nausea. The expensive whiskey Dante and I shared burns twice as much coming back up. My knuckles turn white as I grip the edges, trying to steady myself against the vertigo threatening to pull me under.

Sofia Moretti. My future wife.

The thought sends another violent surge through my gut. I spit and wipe my mouth, pushing back from the toilet to slump against the tiled wall. The bathroom's harsh fluorescent lights make my head pound, but the physical pain is nothing compared to the ache in my chest.

I understand why Dante asked this of me. The logic is sound - a marriage alliance to end generations of bloodshed. To stop the senseless killing. To bring peace between our families. It's the kind of strategic move that has kept the Falchetti family in power for decades.

But fuck, it had to be me.

I close my eyes, but all I see is Elara's face. Her smile when she teased me about my name. The way her wet hair clung to her shoulders after her shower. How her body felt against mine, soft and willing. Perfect.

My fist connects with the wall before I realize I'm moving. The impact sends shockwaves up my arm, but I welcome the pain. It's better than this hollowness spreading through my chest.

"You knew better," I mutter to my reflection in the mirror. Dark circles ring my eyes, and my usually pristine appearance is shot to hell. "You knew she was off limits. You knew this could happen."

But I didn't expect to fall for her. Didn't expect her quick wit or fierce spirit to break through years of carefully constructed walls. Didn't expect to find myself dreaming of a future that could never be.

And now I'm expected to marry her sister. Sofia fucking Moretti. The woman who's been trying to destroy my family. Who's threatened and manipulated and killed her way to power. Just another Mafia Queen who sees marriage as a weapon in her arsenal.

The irony would be funny if it wasn't tearing me apart.

I splash cold water on my face, trying to wash away the bitter taste in my mouth. The wedding will be a sham, of course. A political arrangement nothing more. I'll never touch Sofia, never share her bed. The thought of being intimate with her makes my stomach roll again.

But I'll have to watch as Elara stands beside her sister at the altar. I'll have to pretend I don't see the hurt in her eyes, don't feel the connection between us crackling like electricity. I'll have to act like my heart isn't being ripped from my chest with every false smile and empty promise.

"It's for the family," I tell myself, gripping the edge of the sink. "For peace. For an end to all this."

The words ring hollow in the empty bathroom. Yes, it's for the family. It's always for the family. Every sacrifice, every compromise, every piece of my soul I've had to carve away - all for the greater good of the Falchetti name.

But this... this feels different. This feels like I'm not just sacrificing my happiness, but Elara's too. The memory of her wrapped in that white robe, looking at me like I was something special, something worth loving - it cuts deeper than any knife.

I straighten my tie and smooth back my hair, piece by piece putting my mask back in place. The vulnerable man who spent the night with Elara needs to disappear. In his place must stand the dutiful soldier, the perfect pawn in this game of power and politics.

The bathroom door feels heavier than usual as I push it open. Each step down the hallway is a reminder of what I'm walking away from. What I have to give up.

My phone buzzes in my pocket - probably Dante checking on me. Making sure I haven't run. As if I would. As if I could betray my family like that.

But God, for the first time in my life, I want to. I want to grab Elara and run far from this world of violence and vengeance. Far from arranged marriages and family obligations. Far from everything that's keeping us apart.

Instead, I'll do what I've always done. What I was raised to do. I'll play my part in this tragedy, and I'll do it well. Because that's what it means to be a Falchetti.

Even if it kills me.

epilogue

...

six months later

I stare at my reflection in the ornate mirror of the bride's chamber, hardly recognizing myself. The past months blur together like watercolors bleeding across canvas, each memory tinted with confusion and longing.

My fingers trace the delicate lace trim of my sleeve, remembering that morning three months ago when a stone-faced Falchetti guard appeared at my door in the casino suite. "You're free to go," he'd said, voice devoid of emotion. No explanation. No Luca.

I'd stood there frozen, waiting for him to say more, to tell me where Luca was, why he wasn't there himself. But the guard simply turned and walked away, leaving me alone with a hollowness in my chest that hadn't filled since…

> The black SUV rolls to a stop outside Stilettos, my sister's favorite strip club. My stomach churns at the irony of being dropped here,

like I'm just another piece of disposable entertainment. Through the tinted windows, I spot our guards, weapons raised and ready. My heart pounds against my ribs, but I force myself to breathe steady.

The door swings open and cool night air rushes in. Recognition flashes across the guards' faces and their guns lower in unison. Vinny, one of our most trusted men, extends his hand to help me out. His weathered face shows genuine concern as he scans me for injuries.

"Welcome home, Miss Moretti." His voice is gruff but kind.

I squeeze his hand in silent thanks, letting him guide me through the pulsing neon entrance. The familiar thrum of bass vibrates through my bones as we weave past the main floor. Girls spin and twist on gleaming poles, but I keep my eyes forward. This used to be my playground as a kid, hiding behind the velvet curtains while Sofia handled business. Now it feels like a reminder of everything that's changed.

Vinny leads me through the labyrinth of back hallways, past private rooms and storage closets, to Sofia's office. The door's barely open before she launches herself at me, crushing me in a fierce embrace that knocks the breath from my lungs.

"Thank God," she whispers into my hair. Her arms tighten around me like she's afraid I'll disappear. "I thought I'd lost you."

I cling to her just as desperately, breathing in her familiar perfume. Tears sting my eyes as weeks of fear and loneliness crash over me. My fingers dig into the silk of her blazer. "I missed you so much."

She pulls back just enough to cup my face in her hands, examining every inch like she's cataloging changes. Her dark eyes shine with unshed tears. "Did they hurt you? If they laid a single finger on you, I swear—"

Epilogue

"No," I cut her off quickly. "No, they didn't hurt me." My voice catches as memories of Luca flood back—his gentle touches, passionate kisses, the way he looked at me like I was precious. I push them down deep where they can't betray me. "I'm okay. Really."

Sofia's thumbs brush my cheeks, wiping away tears I didn't realize had fallen. "You're safe now. That's all that matters." She pulls me close again, resting her chin on my head like when we were kids and I'd run to her after nightmares. "I'm never letting you out of my sight again."

I close my eyes and lean into her embrace, trying to find comfort in the familiar scent and warmth of my sister. But my heart aches with the weight of secrets I can never share. How do I tell her that part of me was happiest when I was supposed to be most afraid? That I fell in love with the enemy?

The bass from the club thrums through the walls, a steady rhythm that matches my racing pulse. Sofia's arms around me feel both like home and a cage. I'm back where I belong, but I've never felt more lost.

"There's something you should know," she says finally, pulling back to smooth my hair. "There's something I need to tell you." Her smile is gentle but her eyes are sharp, searching.

My stomach twists. Everything except the truth. Everything except Luca. Everything except the pieces of my heart I left behind in that casino suite.

I force a weak smile and let her guide me toward the private elevator that leads to our penthouse above the club. Each step takes me further from the Falchettis, from Luca, from the girl who dared to dream of a different life. The doors slide shut with a soft ding, and I watch my reflection fragment in the mirrored walls.

"The hairdresser will be here soon to help you girls with your hair," one of the attendants says, breaking through my thoughts. I nod mechanically, my throat too tight to speak.

The window beside me overlooks the cathedral gardens where guests are already gathering. I press my palm against the cool glass, remembering Dante and Lila's wedding six weeks ago. The joy on their faces as they exchanged vows, the way they looked at each other like nothing else in the world existed. I'd searched the crowd that day, hoping to catch a glimpse of dark hair and hazel eyes, but Luca was conspicuously absent.

Had I imagined it all? Those nights in the casino suite, the tender way he'd kissed me, how he'd whispered stories of his childhood against my skin? The connection felt so real, like finding a piece of myself I hadn't known was missing.

Even Enzo and Mia's hasty departure to their Caribbean wedding hasn't dulled the ache. They send occasional photos - sun-kissed and laughing on pristine beaches, their love evident in every casual touch and shared glance. Their happiness should bring me joy, but it only highlights the void in my own heart.

I smooth my hands over the wedding dress hanging on the hook, its pristine white fabric a stark contrast to the darkness swirling inside me. The door creaks open behind me, and I stiffen, expecting Sofia's commanding presence. Instead, my aunt enters, her eyes bright with unshed tears.

"You look beautiful," she whispers, coming to stand beside me. Her fingers brush through my loose curls, just as she did when I was a child. "Are you ready for this?"

Am I ready? The question echoes in my mind, unanswered. *How can I be ready when every fiber of my being screams from nerves? When the mere thought of walking down that aisle makes my stomach churn?*

Epilogue

"I don't understand any of it," I confess, my voice barely audible. "One day I was a prisoner, the next I was free, and now..." I gesture helplessly at my reflection. "It's like I'm watching someone else's life unfold."

My aunt's face softens with sympathy. "Sometimes the path we're meant to walk isn't clear until we're already on it."

I think of Luca again, of the way his eyes would crinkle at the corners when he smiled, how safe I felt in his arms despite being his captive.

The cathedral bells begin to toll, their deep resonance vibrating through the stone walls. Each chime feels like another nail in a coffin, sealing away the dreams I'd barely allowed myself to have.

"It's almost time," my aunt says gently, with trembling hands.

I close my eyes, fighting back tears that threaten to ruin my carefully applied makeup. The weight of expectation presses down on my shoulders like a physical thing. The Moretti name. The family legacy. The carefully orchestrated plans that seem to control every aspect of my life.

Footsteps in the hallway signal Sofia's approach. I take one last look at my reflection, at the stranger wearing a worried face. Somewhere in this vast cathedral, my future awaits. But it's not the future I'd glimpsed in those stolen moments with Luca, not the one I'd begun to hope for in the quiet darkness of the casino suite.

The door opens again, and Sofia sweeps in with her usual air of authority, a hair kit in her hands. "Let's make you perfect," she announces, but I barely hear her...

. . .

THE CATHEDRAL'S vaulted ceiling soars above me, its grandeur almost overwhelming. Sunlight streams through stained glass, casting rainbow patterns across the marble floor where I stand in my white lace gown. My heart pounds against my ribs as I look at the guests filling every pew.

Two families, once bitter enemies, now sit side by side. I watch Moretti men joke with Falchetti soldiers as they pass through metal detectors at the entrance. The sight would have been unthinkable months ago - now they trade playful barbs about whose cooking is better.

The air is thick with the scent of thousands of white roses and lilies. Crystal chandeliers sparkle overhead, and red carpet runs the length of the aisle. Violinists play softly in the corner, their music weaving through the excited murmurs of hundreds of guests in their finest suits and gowns.

Traditional Italian wedding cookies and Jordan almonds wrapped in tulle sit at each place setting. The ancient cathedral has been transformed into a wonderland of white and gold, with flowing fabric draped between marble columns. It's exactly how I dreamed my wedding would be, even if the circumstances that brought us here were unexpected.

As I stand at the altar beside Luca, his hand warm in mine, I can hardly believe this moment is real. His dark eyes meet mine with such tenderness as we exchange our vows. This may have started as a political arrangement, but my heart swells with genuine love for this man...

> *My mind drifts back to that day Sofia told me she would marry Luca to forge peace between our families. I'd never felt such despair —or such determination. Through my tears, I'd confessed everything to her. How I had fallen in love with him during my*

Epilogue

captivity, and how the thought of him marrying someone else was unbearable. But now, the stakes were even higher.

"Sofia," I said, my voice trembling, "there's something else you need to know. I'm pregnant." The words hung in the air, a heavy weight between us. "Luca is the father."

Sofia's expression shifted, shock filling her eyes as she processed my confession. "I love him, Sofia. I can't let him marry someone else; it would break me. I want to marry him myself. I want to be the bridge between our families, not just as your sister, but as Luca's wife."

She studied me carefully, a storm of emotions flickering across her face as she searched for the truth in my eyes. After what felt like an eternity, she pulled me into her arms, whispering, "If this is what you truly want, little sister, then I can't stand in your way."

Now here we stand, Luca sliding a diamond ring onto my finger as he promises to love and cherish me forever. When the priest pronounces us husband and wife, Luca cups my face in his hands and kisses me with such passion that the guests erupt in whistles and applause.

I catch glimpses of our families as we turn to face them—Dante and Lila beaming from the front row, Sofia dabbing at her eyes with a handkerchief, Giovanni nodding in approval. The feud that claimed so many lives is finally over.

As Luca leads me back down the aisle, rose petals raining down around us, I see not just the joining of two people, but the birth of something greater. The Moretti and Falchetti families united to create an empire spanning the continent, and soon our baby—the first to carry both bloodlines—will bridge our families forever. Luca's hand rests protectively over my growing belly as we walk, and in this moment, all I care about is the way he squeezes my other hand and the love shining in his eyes when he looks at me.

This marriage may have been arranged to forge an alliance, but fate had other plans. Sometimes the most powerful bonds are formed in the most unexpected ways.

THE END

you might also like

the dark side of him

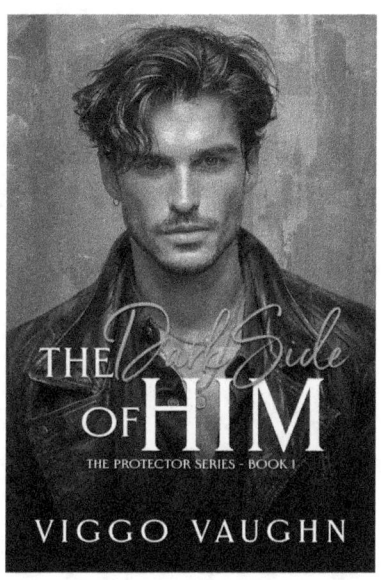

love ignites. loyalty crumbles. danger explodes.

Lila Rossi, an artist with a thirst for life, gets tangled in a deadly underworld war after witnessing a brutal mob hit. Now, she's a target, and the ruthless enforcer **Dante Falchetti** is her only protection.

Dante is a man of shadows with a past as dark as his suits. He's bound by duty, yet Lila's fiery spirit sparks an unexpected flame.

Lila: Trapped in a world of violence, she finds solace in the forbidden allure of her protector. But can love bloom amidst the threat of mob executions?

As danger escalates, the line between protector and desired blurs.

Can they survive the storm brewing around them, or will their secrets and desires consume them both?

Delve into a world of

- Gritty Mob Warfare
- Steamy Forbidden Romance
- Heart-stopping Suspense

The Protector Series - Book 1

Ebook & Paperback

guarded by shadows

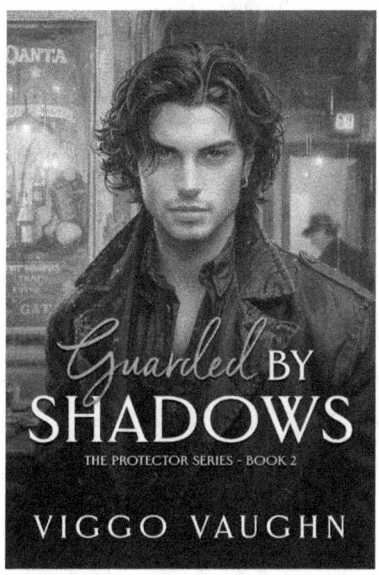

she witnessed a mob secret. now, a dangerous heir is her only protector.

Mia Ricci, a ray of sunshine at the local diner, stumbles upon a dangerous secret. When the witness disappears, Mia becomes the target. Enter **Enzo Falchetti**, the captivating heir to a mafia empire, tasked with guarding the woman who could shatter his world.

But duty and desire clash.

As they navigate a world of threats and hidden agendas, their initial wariness melts into a passionate bond. Can Enzo protect Mia from the shadows that threaten to consume them both? Will he choose love or the legacy he's sworn to uphold?

Dive into *Guarded by Shadows*, a sizzling tale of forbidden love, mob suspense, and a bodyguard who'll risk everything.

The Protector Series - Book 2

Ebook & Paperback

the bargain bride

By V. Vaughn

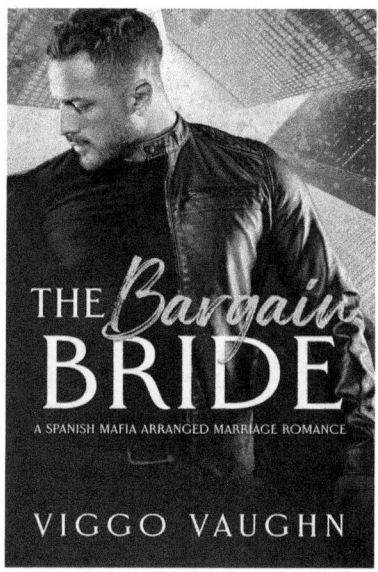

grease, grit, and a dangerous proposition

Chelsea Jenkins is a woman who knows how to fix a flat tire and a failing business. But when a notorious **Mafia heir** sets up shop across the street, sparks fly hotter than a welding torch.

Victor Morales is all about fast cars, loose women, and keeping his father's criminal empire humming. The last thing he needs is a fiery mechanic throwing wrenches in his plans.

But desperation has a way of changing the game. When Chelsea stumbles upon a shocking secret, Victor makes her an offer she can't refuse.

Love? Never part of the deal.

Survival? A high-octane gamble.

The Bargain Bride is a story where danger simmers beneath the grease, and love takes a reckless turn for the unexpected.

Get ready for a wild ride!

A Spanish Mafia Arranged Marriage Romance
Ebook & Paperback

second in command

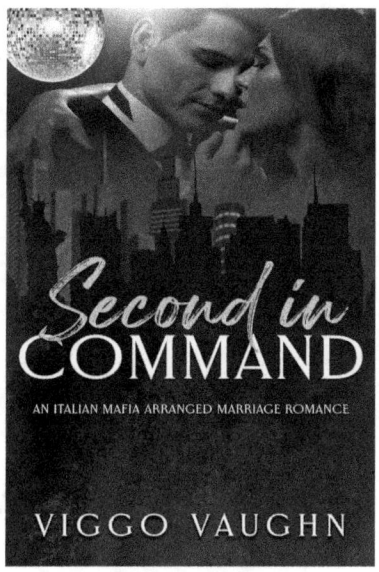

1977 new york

Francesca Donato was twenty-one, and in her prime. Gorgeous, wild, an Italian princess. Her father, second in command under Vincenzio Benedetti the *Capo* of the Montagna Mafia family, spoiled his daughter to extremes where she always got what she wanted. Designer clothes, exotic cars and money, Francesca wanted Enzo, a soldier in the Benedetti army.

Enzo Andonetto was untamed, out of control and trigger happy. Nightclubs, dancing and drugs were always on the menu when he spotted Francesca dancing one night at the club with her friends.

Apart, they were lively, but together, they were a force, and Vincenzio welcomed their union when Enzo asked his permission to marry her. But there was one test the Capo needed Enzo to do before his wedding, get rid of a rival that was stealing from their territory.

How does an unmatched pair climax? By violence, and an unexpected gunshot that came from nowhere…

An Italian Mafia Arranged Marriage Romance

Includes crossover characters from "*Evenly Matched*"

Ebook & Paperback

evenly matched

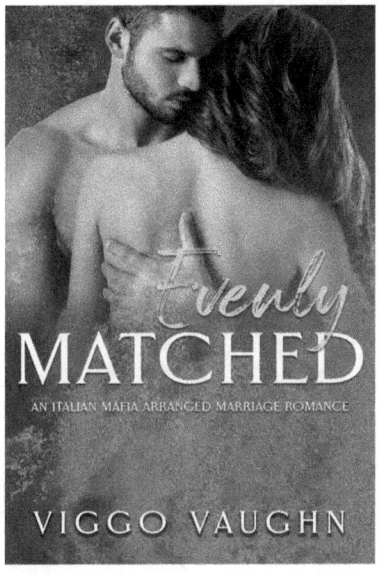

Lorenzo Beneditti was his mother's favorite but his father's constant source of trouble. The Beneditti family was well known throughout many organized crime families; they were considered top-level, the peak of the Italian Mob. At twenty-two, Lorenzo repeatedly tried to live up to his father's expectations but always fell short—until he met his match in the female version of himself.

Carla Caldarelli was her father's favorite but her mother's worst nightmare. The Caldarelli family were soldiers of the Beneditti's—second in command—so when Carla finds herself in a bind, she looks to Lorenzo for help.

Can Lorenzo save Carla? Can Carla rescue Lorenzo?

Includes crossover characters from *"The Bargain Bride"*

An Italian Mafia Arranged Marriage Romance

Ebook & Paperback

about viggo vaughn

Viggo Vaughn is an emerging author of Mafia Romance, Mystery/Suspense and Thrillers. Viggo has many writing interests and lives an incognito digital lifestyle.

Viggo is part of the Ardent Artist Books family and is currently the author of several books.

youtube.com/theardentartist

amazon.com/stores/Ardent-Artist-Books/author/B08BX8F1DZ

also by viggo vaughn

CROSSOVER•CHARACTERS

The Bargain Bride - Book 1

Evenly Matched - Book 2

Second in Command - Book 3

THE•PROTECTOR•SERIES

The Dark Side of Him - Book 1

Guarded by Shadows - Book 2

Tangled Loyalties - Book 3

www.ingramcontent.com/pod-product-compliance
Lightning Source LLC
LaVergne TN
LVHW010328070526
838199LV00065B/5690